What Mama Said

OTHER CREATIVE WORKS
BY OSONYE TESS ONWUEME

Shakara: Dance-Hall Queen. San Francisco: African Heritage Press, 2000. *Winner, the 2001 Association of Nigerian Authors (ANA) Drama Prize.

Why the Elephant Has No Butt. San Francisco: African Heritage Press, 2000.

Tell It to Women. Detroit: Wayne State University Press, 1997. *Winner, the 1995 Association of Nigerian Authors (ANA) Drama Prize.

Riot in Heaven. San Francisco: African Heritage Press, 1997.

The Missing Face. San Francisco: African Heritage Press, 1996.

Three Plays. Detroit: Wayne State University Press, 1993.

Legacies. Ibadan: Heinemann Nigeria Ltd., 1989.

The Reign of Wazobia. Ibadan: Heinemann Nigeria Ltd., 1988.

Mirror for Campus. Ibadan: Heinemann Nigeria Ltd., 1987.

Ban Empty Barn and Other Plays. Ibadan: Heinemann Nigeria Ltd., 1986.

The Desert Encroaches. Ibadan: Heinemann Nigeria Ltd., 1995. *Winner, the 1985 Association of Nigerian Authors (ANA) Drama Prize.

The Broken Calabash. Ibadan: Heinemann Nigeria Ltd., 1984.

A Hen Too Soon. Owerri: Heins Nigeria Publishers, 1983.

What Mama Said

AN EPIC DRAMA

Osonye Tess Onwueme

Introduction by
Maureen N. Eke

Wayne State University Press
Detroit

African American Life Series

A COMPLETE LISTING OF THE BOOKS IN THIS SERIES CAN BE
FOUND AT THE BACK OF THIS VOLUME.

Series Editors:

Melba Joyce Boyd
Department of Africana Studies, Wayne State University

Ron Brown
Department of Political Science, Wayne State University

Library of Congress Cataloging-in-Publication Data

Onwueme, Osonye Tess.
    What mama said : an epic drama / Osonye Tess Onwueme ; introduction by
Maureen N. Eke.
        p. cm. — (African American life series)
    ISBN 0-8143-3141-6 (alk. paper)
    1. Petroleum industry and trade—Drama.   2. Government, Resistance to—
Drama.   3. Political corruption—Drama.   4. Africa—Drama.   I. Title.
II. Series.
    PR9387 .9.O537W475 2003
    822' .914—dc21

                                                          2003003894

∞ The paper used in this publication meets the minimum requirements of the
American National Standard for Information Sciences—Permanence of Paper for
Printed Library Materials, ANSI Z39.48-1984.

for you
NONSO
gone . . .
too soon . . . too soon . . .
gone . . .

much too soon!

but for me
for mama
for kim
and oh for many many others
I know
You still live
and will live
on forever

NONSO

K'omesi-o!
peace. peace. peace.

INTRODUCTION: WHO SHALL SILENCE
THE DRUMS? ANOTHER WOMEN'S WAR

Nigerian-born dramatist Osonye Tess Onwueme has established her reputation as one of the leading black female playwrights in Africa and the United States today. Onwueme has also carved out a niche for herself as a cultural interpreter and an investigator of African women's lives, gender politics, and the impact of transnational or global politics on the lives of the underrepresented, especially women, children, and the impoverished masses. With about fifteen plays to her credit, each of which addresses an issue of social concern, she has reactivated the idea of the engaged artist, the committed artist, who like the griot of African oral narratives retells or creates new stories about the community and its leaders. Also like the griot or oral historian, she critiques her society, forcing it to reexamine itself. Onwueme has continued the Nigerian theatrical and literary tradition of social commitment led and perfected by one of her teachers, Wole Soyinka. Like Soyinka's works, *Kongi's Harvest, A Dance of the Forests,* and his prison diary, *The Man Died,* which provided the international community with a caustic criticism of postcolonial Nigeria, Onwueme's works are strident criticisms of Nigeria, but they are seen specifically through women's lenses, a perspective not provided by Soyinka.

Onwueme describes herself as a writer whose perspective is informed by multinational, multicultural, and historical, including African diasporic, experiences. In fact, Onwueme's perspective is becoming increasingly pan-African as the African diasporic legacy becomes a dominant theme in several of her plays, including *The Missing Face, Riot in Heaven,* and *Shakara.* But this expanding perspective has not deterred her from directing her lenses at postcolonial Nigeria. In her newest play, *What Mama Said,* she focuses on the effect of national and global oil politics on the lives of women, youth, and impoverished rural Nigerians.

In 2000, she received a Ford Foundation research grant for her project "Who Can Silence the Drums? Delta Women Speak!" The project examines the lives of rural women of the oil-producing regions of the Niger Delta in

Nigeria. Her play *What Mama Said* is a product of that project. In this play Onwueme returns to a perennial theme, the disempowerment of rural women, those who "till the land, those who have the power to make and unmake the land." As an advocate for women, particularly Nigeria's rural women, whose lives she introduced to us in her epic *Tell It to Women,* Onwueme allows women to take center stage in this play. Again, she explores their disenfranchisement by tyrannical cultural practices and traditions, class, gender, postcolonial national and international politics. In an attempt to give women voice and to imbue their lives with meaning, Onwueme creates combatant female characters who confront those structures that seek to subordinate them. In this new play, Omi, Imo, and Hadeja, her young female protagonists, galvanize their mothers under a battle cry of land reclamation. "Our land! We must-must take back what is ours! Resource Control," the women scream, insisting on their ownership of the land and the nation, asserting "We have no leaders!"

The dilemma of rural women in a postcolonial Nigeria driven by a New World Order of global politics is not foreign to Onwueme. In fact, it is the primary focus of her play *Tell It to Women,* where Ruth and Daisy, her middle-class Western-educated women, ironically subordinate the very women whose lives they aspire to transform through the government-sanctioned urban-based "Better life for rural women's" program. Like *Tell It to Women, What Mama Said* is also a scathing criticism of the national leadership's abdication of its responsibility to the citizens it has promised to protect. Whereas in *Tell It to Women,* the rural women confront the city and those elite women who claim to speak for them, in *What Mama Said,* the women do not have representatives; no one speaks for them. Like their foremothers, who protested against the British colonial administration's taxation during the "Aba women's war" (1928–30), the women in Onwueme's play rise in mass protest against a combination of oppressive forces: multinational oil companies with neo-imperial intentions and corrupt local/national leaders, who have abdicated their responsibilities. In addition, Onwueme's play invokes a number of women's rebellions of the 1980s against multinational oil corporations, which have polluted farmlands and alienated women, who are the primary cultivators of farmlands, from their lands. For instance, in 1984 and 1986, women rose in Ogharefe and Ughelli (former Bendel, now Delta State), respectively, in protest against what they saw as the exploitative presence of foreign oil corporations, which not only had alienated them from their lands but also had not compensated them adequately. In fact, the Ughelli LGA women's revolt began as a localized protest against the taxation of women but gradually transformed into a mass revolt against the loss of fishing and farm lands, oil pollution, the lack of compensation for lost lands, and unequal distribution of oil wealth. In the 1990s, Ogoni women mobilized and rebelled against the presence of multinational oil corporations on their lands.

These are the issues against which Onwueme's women protest. In the opening scene of "Movement Nine," Oshimi and Cross River, two major rivers of Nigeria, now personified as leading female figures, cry out against the death of the land and call other women to action. Calling the mothers and daughters of the land, Oshimi informs them of a threat to their land, their soul, stating, "Something . . . something strange, smelly, and strong is sapping our land." Her sister, Cross River, adds, "People of Sufferland! Our land bleeds! The land weeps! Tell me, who among you here, no matter how young, no matter how old, has not lost our blood?" In a call-and-response sequence led by Cross River's urging questions, the chorus of women, now frenzied by their anguish and loss, chant the many atrocities they and their families have experienced:

> Cross River: Your fathers and brothers?
> Chorus: Lost, branded, or wounded!
> Cross River: Your mothers and sisters?
> Chorus (Inflamed): Defied, maimed, or murdered!
> Cross River: Your pride and dignitiy?
> Chorus: Cut down!
> Cross River: And if they take all away, and what is left?
> Chorus: Nothing! Nothing!

While these questions and their responses delineate the women's personal experiences, the effect is a collective awakening to their shared reality, which helps to galvanize them into an oppositional body. Again, Cross River declares, "Ever since they discovered oil in our land, they drill, dry, and fry us with the fishes and farmlands all cooking in oil." Then, she asks, "Do you smell the fishes roasting in their hot oil poured over the rivers?" to which the chorus of women responds, "Yes! They've refined our oil into a curse!" Punning on the word "refine," the women signal the transformation of oil, perceived initially as a gift, an economic "blessing," into a potential source of their demise. The significance of the pun is also not lost on Cross River, who, appropriating their symbolism, asks, "Where? Where else in the world does oil cease to anoint?" "Here! Here! Here!" the women scream. Again, Cross River prompts them, providing another catalog of losses: "Plants, animals, children, men, women cooking in their oil. Oil sapped from the very soul of our sagging land. Ah! People of Sufferland! Do you see yourselves drowning?" "Yes!" the women shout. At the end, whipped into a fury, the women rise to action, shouting, "No more waiting!" and as the stage direction indicates, "in this fury, the mob rises, facing the direction of the GRA/Oil Club."

Onwueme is quite aware of the powerful political messages of this play. It draws attention to the national and international silences over the impoverishment of Nigerians, especially those from the oil-producing areas of the country. The play also draws attention to the loss of rich farmlands to large oil multinational corporations and the complicity of Nigerian local and national governments in the perpetration of environmental violence against Nigerians, especially in the Niger Delta. It is for articulating such opposition that writer-activist Ken Saro-Wiwa lost his life. On November 10, 1995, he was executed by the Nigerian military government, despite international protests, for his opposition to the illegal appropriation and environmental destruction of Ogoni farm lands by multinational oil corporations, the lack of compensation to the Ogoni, and the murder of Ogoni people.[1] He had founded the Movement for the Survival of Ogoni People (MOSOP) as a means of organizing his people to fight against environmental destruction and to demand their rights by drawing local and international attention to their subordination by multinational oil corporations in collusion with the Nigerian government. As Rob Nixon points out in "Environmental Justice and Microminority Rights,"

> By the time Saro-Wiwa was executed, the Nigerian military and Mobile Police Force had killed 2,000 Ogoni through direct murder and the burning of villages. Ogoni air had been fouled by the flaring of natural gas; Ogoni croplands scarred by oil spills; Ogoni drinking and fishing waters poisoned. Although Shell was driven out of Ogoniland in 1993, it simply moved on to the other parts of Nigeria's once lush delta, now a delta of death. (111)

Clearly, these are the problems that Onwueme's women confront and march against in the play. But environmental injustice is not their only concern; they also rage against the poor economy, the absence of jobs for the youth, and in general the greed and unaccountability of their leaders. "We reject all leaders of falsehood. We reject leaders who take and take and never give anything good in return! Away! Away with their lies!" they scream. Had this play been written during the military dictatorship that executed Saro-Wiwa, Onwueme would have been described as unpatriotic and possibly charged with treason. She would also have been persecuted or faced a similar fate as Saro-Wiwa, imprisonment, or exile, linking her with a number of African writers, including Dennis Brutus, Jack Mapanje, Nawal el Saadawi, Wole Soyinka, and Ngugi wa Thiong'o, to mention only a few.

Only international attention to their cause will give Onwueme's women solace. Led by the youth, they assert their agency by abducting representatives of the international oil corporations, the local leaders, and several national political figures. In the mock court scene of the epilogue, convened to try the women and youth, it is ironically the leaders who are on trial—hence the title "A Nation in Custody." In collapsing the identities of several figures—the Supreme Court is now led by oppressive characters such as Oceana, the foreign oil representative, and Pipeline, the corrupt local businessman and chief—Onwueme succeeds in signaling a continuity in the hierarchies and relations of power. Those who have controlled the resources continue to cling to and desire to exert power over the women and youth, whom they have disempowered. The public, however, outraged by the women's detention, demands their freedom. In the trial scene, it becomes clear that the nation and its leadership rather than the women and youth are on trial. Hadeja (one of the young girls), now as defense attorney for the accused women, draws attention to the women's victimization by cataloging the wrongs they have suffered when she says:

> For nearly half a century, Your Honor, the living mothers, sons, and daughters of the land have been trampled. Oppressed. Exploited. And dehumanized. . . . Since the Sweet Crude was discovered in their land, each one of them has had their own personal tragic experiences. They've been without jobs, farming and fishing resources . . . painful, hard experiences that progressively changed their lives for the worse.

In presenting their stories of tragedy, alienation, and dehumanization before a world court, Hadeja helps them to claim their humanity and voices, which are slowly being muted. "I cannot speak for them!" Hadeja announces to the court. "Let them speak," she adds. Calling the women, she urges them: "Now it's time! Your time. Speak for yourselves! Speak." Like Brecht's Saint Joan of the Stockyards, these young women—Hadeja, Imo, and Omi—pick up the mantle of leadership to lead the charge against new forces of oppression. They are the catalyst for their mothers' rebellion, for in the opening scene of the play, a young woman asks, "Don't you think it's time? Time to take our case to the people . . . In short, the world?"

"Land is life," Pipeline ironically tells us early in the play. Generations of Africans have died in their struggles against the loss of their indigenous lands. The landscapes of African national and continental histories "from Cape Town to Cairo" are littered with the bodies of Africans lost in the struggles to preserve African lands. A people or nation without its lands is no nation. Hence, national liberation struggles as well as several post-independent civil wars have been waged over land issues. Ironically, it is the land that suffers. For Nigerians, Biafra and the civil war are painful reminders of the struggle over the control of the land and resources. Still, more than thirty years after Biafra, these issues continue to dominate national discussions. The women's protest in Onwueme's play underscores the need for a national discussion of the abuse of power by the leadership and its representatives as well as the marginalization or eliding of particular groups. Saro-Wiwa and his MOSOPs reminded us, as do Onwueme's women, of this need to struggle against annihilation by neo-imperial forces.

Although women are at the center of this play, Onwueme carefully avoids a vilification of men. In fact, the women work with the youth whose leadership is composed of young men and young women. Women, however, are the dominant figures. One can attribute their dominance to a number of factors. The protest begins at the market square, and because women generally control the market, it is not surprising that the protest's leadership is in the hands of women. In addition, they are marginalized and victimized in multiple ways, by patriarchial structures (Pipeline, Imo's uncle, gives her to a white man in exchange for oil "Deals") and by the failing economy, which affects their market economy. At the beginning of the play and in the beginning of "Movement Four," Hawker/Hadeja is seen desperately trying to sell her fruit without success. Most men, especially in these oil-producing regions, have gone to work in the refineries, leaving the women and children behind.

As a dramatist who is also interested in interpreting and promoting African cultural practices, Onwueme infuses her plays with African—more specifically, Nigerian-cultural practices. Dance and songs are integral features of this play, eliciting comparisons with Ngugi wa Thiong'o's *I Will Marry When I Want.* Much of the movement of the play is driven by the women's protest marches, which utilize chants and dances. As in her earlier works (masquarade dance and praise poetry in *Wazobia* and *The Missing Face*; reggae, rap, and hip-hop in *Shakara*; gospel, blues, and the spirituals in *Riot in Heaven*), Onwueme returns to her reservoir of cultural memory for forms that affirm her status as a dramatist.

Clearly, Onwueme has established herself as one of Nigeria's, if not Africa's, most prolific and engaged playwrights. As an advocate for women, children, and the masses, whom she says have been muted by traditional, national, and transnational politics and relations, Onwueme has written a play that, like her other plays, is a platform from which the voiceless can speak. Indeed, reading or experiencing any of Onwueme's plays is an excursion into a wide range of social, political, historical, and cultural encounters. Her plays are contributions to larger national, African, and pan-African or international discussions of gender, race, history, and politics (national and global). In this play, the focus is the women's presentation of their stories, and, as Imo says, all the women want is to "live with dignity," to tell their own stories.

Professor Maureen N. Eke
Central Michigan University

NOTE

1. See Maureen N. Eke, "The Novel: *Sozaboy:* A Novel in Rotten English," in *Ken Saro-Wiwa: Writer and Political Activist,* ed. Craig W. McLuckie and Aubrey McPhail (Boulder: Lynne Rienner Publishers, 2000), 87–106. See also Rob Nixon's "Pipe Dreams: Ken Saro-Wiwa, Environmental Justice, and Microminority," 109–25, in the same edited volume.

What Mama Said

PRODUCTION HISTORY OF THE DRAMA

With generous financial support of the Ford Foundation in 2000–2001, *What Mama Said* was first staged at the State Cultural Centre, Calabar, Cross-River State, Nigeria, on July 6, 2001, with actors and crew members from the Nigerian Theatre Guild. Though the play was subsequently adopted for Command Performances by the Delta State Government, and was directed by David Orere, the following were the original cast and crew who toured the major cities of the Niger-Delta states with the production:

THE CAST

OMI	Amina Joda
OCEANA	Bassey Ekpo Bassey
PIPELINE	Sunday Umana
OSHIMI	Affiong Okon
CROSS RIVER	Eme Ekanem Enyamba
IMO	Ekakem Ekpenyong
HADEJA	Nsa Honesty
YOBE	Thomas Etuk
BONNY	Norman Do Noor

DRUMMERS/ACTIVISTS

Ufford Ikike	Raymond Inyang
Archibong E. Asibong	Morris Bassey
Victor Thompson	Ita Okon

THE TECHNICAL CREW

Artistic Director	Chris Nwamuo
Lighting & Sceneography	Molinta Enendu

Choreography	Raymond Inyang
Costumes	Margaret Akpan
Make-Up	Ann Okon
Publicity	Itoro-Obing Etuk
Stage Manager	Jide Ogunkilede
Sound	Pius Kumengisa
Property Master	Hilary Elemi

THE SETTING

All actions take place in the fictional State of Sufferland. There are two main activity areas. One is marked the GRA/OIL CLUB, with the sign: RESTRICTED AREA. KEEP OFF! A locked iron gate shields this restricted area, with all its nuances of affluence and upper-class habitation. Opposite this area is the bare surrounding of the Market-Square, which is the main frontier of the community's life activity and struggle. There are no solid structures to inhibit the flow of the people's movement. Only the barricaded empty fuel station stands out in this open marketplace.

CHARACTERS IN THE PLAY

Please note that a number of the fictional characters in this play are named after rivers or bodies of water, both big and small. While the smaller waters act as youths, evolving and changing roles, the bigger ones remain fairly constant, even in their dynamic change of courses. Note, too, that when the lead actors are not engaged in specific roles, they join the rest of the restless crowd as youths. Though some individual characters might play significantly important or dominant roles, the drama is not specifically about them. Rather, like the swift currents of water that defy limiting boundaries (or "arrests"!), these Promethean characters both embody and project the dynamic change or movement that transforms the life and consciousness of a people, hanging on the cliff of existence and power.

In the enduring legacy of their British colonial heritage, the indigenous language, which the local inhabitants would normally speak, has been translated into standard English language. However, as it does occur in real life situations in postcolonial Nigeria today, these characters frequently ease into the more popular Pidgin, as well as the indigenous language, either in the more informal or familiar contexts, or as a way of signalling social class inequality and difference in specific contexts.

Imo: The 27-year-old niece of PIPELINE is an unemployed schoolteacher, who grows into a militant force in the people's movement.

Oshimi: She's a 45-year-old widow and leader of the market women. With her unemployed, restless children and militant youths, she takes strides in leading her people's struggle for change.

Cross River: With her friend OSHIMI and the militant youths, the 43-year-old widow and mother leads the market women and the people's struggle.

Omi: She's the 23-year-old rebellious daughter of OSHIMI and mistress of the foreign Oil Director (OCEANA). Though well educated, she's unemployed. Worse still, she feels rebuffed by her white master (OCEANA) and then grows into the beacon of her people's revolutionary struggle for change.

Hadeja: She's the 20-year-old unemployed daughter of OSHIMI and younger sister of OMI. A good friend of IMO, she works as a Hawker/Seller and plays a leading role in the struggle.

Yobe: He is the Government Official. He plays the role of POLICE OFFICER ONE.

Pipeline: He is the Traditional Chief, who is in close alliance with YOBE and OCEANA. He plays the role of TRIAL JUSTICE and BUSINESSMAN.

Oceana: He's the powerful foreign Oil Director and a close ally of both YOBE and PIPELINE. OMI is his mistress. He plays the role of GENERAL.

Bonny: He is an unemployed youth. He plays the role of POLICE OFFICER THREE, GUARD X, PROSECUTOR, OLD MAN, and PRIEST.

Ikpoba: Also known as the Bandit-Boy, this young man is Omi's Lover and Cross River's son. He takes a job as one of Oceana's security guards (Guard Y). He plays the role of POLICE OFFICER TWO, JOBLESS MAN, and FUEL ATTENDANT

PROLOGUE

(The action begins now at the dark center of the village Market-Square. The space looks bare, tired, and sleepy, except for the glowing crescent moon, hanging in one corner of the dominant indigo sky. At first, a strident drumbeat greets the world, but it is soon silenced by the avalanche of gunshots, explosive sounds, war drums, and angry voices descending on this tired land. In the shadows, a sudden shrieking sound follows as two limping, terrified young women flee from locations in the audience to center stage. Wounded and out of breath, they support, nurse, and comfort each other until they break into a spiritual/blues song. Still in the shadows, two frightened youths (male and female) who are fleeing from some invisible assailants come crashing on them with their shouts: "They're coming again! Help! Save us! They'll kill us! Help! Help! Save us!" The young women try their best to help until the number of refugees swells beyond their power to control, with the wounded, including the older women, gathering there to seek refuge. All around, they continue to comfort and nurse the traumatized, crying out loud: "They took her . . . tore her up right before me." "See! See what they're doing to me at my age!" an old woman cries out. "You too, mother? Aaaah!" And another, "They killed him . . . shot him point-blank right before me!" "Just like they did to my husband and son!" another wails.

Suddenly, sirens slash through their tired voices as heavily armed men storm the scene from all directions, forcing this wounded community into a more alarming, urgent race for life and survival. They try to flee in different directions, but a youth is captured and held hostage as the others escape. For a while, thick shrouds of silence drape the land, until one by one, they start to reemerge, angry, defiant, determined to be no longer crippled with fear or silence. With everyone gathering, soothing and holding on to the other, they slowly form a human chain until they break into songs of solidarity. The first fugitive youths have become so animated by their experience, they lead the people's song, and provoke them into dialogue with the audience. The drama has begun.)

YOUNG WOMAN:
You see? It's how it's been with us. See? Now tell me, how long can anyone continue like this?

CHORUS:
How long? How long?

YOUNG WOMAN:
Don't you think it's time? Time to take our case to the people . . . In short, the world?

CHORUS:
Yes, People of the world! Hear! Hear! Hear us and judge for yourselves!

WOMAN:
Not our blood for oil.

CHORUS:
No! Not our blood for oil.

WOMAN:
Now women, beat, beat the drums!

YOUNG WOMAN:
What did Mama say?

CHORUS:
(*Pounding their feet.*) Beat! Beat! Beat the drums! (*Drumbeats rise.*) Beat! Beat! Beat the drums!

YOUNG WOMAN:
What Mama said-What Mama said . . .

CHORUS:
(*Breaking into dance.*) Women, beat, beat the drums!

YOUNG WOMAN:
And so she said it: Not our blood for oil!

CHORUS:
Women, beat! Beat! Beat the drums!

(*With unified rhythms, and creeping to center stage, the victims break into vibrant dance-steps. Meanwhile, the Young Woman quickly exits behind and returns with a box full of clothing, household items, and whatever else is required to dramatize their experience. The people are so animated that in no time, the items are all organized or distributed and they dress up for their new roles. Thus transformed, some begin to mime and adjust to their new characters/personalities, while others set up the stage. Once the stage is set, they quickly hold hands, form a human chain or shield as they continue their vibrant dance/chant, pounding the earth with their feet. Suddenly a loud explosion shatters their world. Chaos breaks loose as the people scream and flee in all directions. Blackout. The drama has entered another stage.*)

MOVEMENT ONE

(Right side of the Market-Square. It's a hot afternoon in the GRA/Oil Club. Seated, and playing a game of Monopoly around a lounge table with a white canopy above it are the powerful allies: OCEANA as the foreign Director of the oil club, YOBE, the national Government Official of oil, and PIPELINE, the Traditional Chief. A large TV screen mounted above broadcasts the day's news reports. An empty chair, a stool with a speakerphone set on one side and a radio with drinking glasses on the other mark Oceana's space from his partners. The men remain absorbed in their game until the TV anchorman directly presents the angry protesting mob: "We can't wait! We won't wait! Enough is enough! We can't wait! We won't wait!" This irritates OCEANA, and he quickly switches off the radio, cursing under his breath: "Damn! These people! There we go again!" He lights a cigarette, presses the speakerphone, and calls out: "More service!" OMI quickly steps out from inside. Her red short skirt and sleeveless blouse taunt the eyes, announcing her agile, youthful body mounted above platform shoes. Like a seasoned waitress, she bears a tray of alcoholic drinks and glasses. She greets the men, bends down to serve them, with their greedy eyes marking the geography of her body. OCEANA is most affected; he quickly loses interest in the game, pulls her into his bosom, and sends his hands to work and wander around her willing body. Meanwhile, his equally distracted partners try to sustain the game.)

YOBE:
Man, that's some deep, deep waters you're in. Mind you get drowned. *(They chuckle. Each pushes his own game forward.)*

PIPELINE:
Yes. Easy. Take care, my friend.

OCEANA:
(To OMI.) Deep, sweetie. More, baby. More! *(Lifts his glass, toasts.)*

OMI:
To you. I'm at your service.

OCEANA:
My express service from Venus! *(OMI responds with a smile.)* Not so?

23

OMI:
(*Smiling seductively.*) One thing you got right!

OCEANA:
Yeah. My special brew from Sufferland! Let's drink to that.
(*He toasts, this time with the men. PIPELINE obeys but appears uncomfortable with the apparent vulgarity. Still fondling.*) You belong to me, Babe.

OMI:
Now.

OCEANA:
Sure. (*Yawns, runs fingers through hair.*) So unruly. Babe, I need . . .

OMI:
(*Leaving.*) A clean shave.

OCEANA:
You got it.

OMI:
(*Smiling seductively.*) Yes. Play on. I'll soon be back.

(*She picks up the empty glass, steps back seductively into the door. Her sister, HADEJA, appears as the Hawker/Seller with IKPOBA/JOBLESS MAN. She's carrying a fruit basket on her head, while IKPOBA/JOBLESS MAN is armed with his machete. At the gate they break into a call-response chant: "Buy pawpaw! Sweet like Sugar! Buy my pawpaw!" Then IKPOBA/JOBLESS MAN throws up his machete, flips and turns it into a javelin as he chants: "I Sabi cut grass! Try me! I fit cut grass! And fertilizer? I fit put am too! Just try me! Oga try me!" When he stops, HADEJA takes over. OCEANA simply gives them a spiteful look and curses under his breath: "These lazy bastards!" In response, YOBE says, "Can't trust any of them. Just a bunch of nuisances. Let's play, my friend." That said, the men resume their game. Tired of being ignored, the solicitors leave.*)

OCEANA:
(*Turns to PIPELINE and YOBE.*) Should I trust her?

PIPELINE:
Who?

OCEANA:
The girl . . .

YOBE:
Omi? But why not?

OCEANA:
You know . . . these people . . . Well, I don't know. We'll see.

PIPELINE:
Hmm . . . I'll tell you what the monkey said about trust. "I tell you I can trust the baby that I'm still carrying in my womb. The one behind my back, well, how can I tell?"

OCEANA:
Interesting. So . . .?

PIPELINE:
Don't misunderstand me. I know her . . . I mean, her mother, leader of the market women.

OCEANA:
I guess you do. You *know* every woman in the entire region.

PIPELINE:
I try. (*Silence.*) Believe me, nobody from the other side or tribe will dare to come . . . I mean cross the line.

YOBE:
True. The boundary is marked with fire. Can't you hear them?

(*They listen. Angry voices of the community, screaming: "Commot! Go! Go back to your land. No! You can't continue to take the jobs when we're here. Go! They already gave you people the local government headquarters. What else do you want? To take everything? OK here? Come and drink all the oil with your oyibo! You dogs of the White man!"*)

OCEANA:
You hear that? Everyday, war. Agitation. The pipelines are no longer safe. We're losing money . . . Losing staff . . . Drilling oil here is fast becoming a dangerous business. (*Pause.*) Hmm . . . Omi. I wonder why she's taking so long. What is she up to now?

YOBE:
Maybe taking her time for her make up. You know them . . .

PIPELINE:
Women? Inflammable . . . Hazards . . . Ha!

OCEANA:
(*Rising.*) Let's see . . .
(*He disappears behind the closed door. YOBE and PIPELINE are now alone.*)

PIPELINE:
You know he's right.

YOBE:
Yes. But we're also doing our best.

PIPELINE:
And our best's not good enough?

YOBE:
Maybe. But then, where do we go from here?

PIPELINE:
Just last week, the Deputy Director of hell . . .

YOBE:
Shell, you mean?

PIPELINE:
Oh, well . . . you know what I mean? The Shell Vice . . .

OCEANA:
(*Returning.*) Yes, poor Jack! You know my deputy narrowly escaped from those hooligans?

PIPELINE:
So we heard.

OCEANA:
(*Sighs.*) Who knows what they're going to do next?

YOBE:
And now they're poaching in the oil pipelines just because of their greed and . . .

OCEANA:
(*Drinks.*) Set the damn thing ablaze!

YOBE:
In the Jesse-Delta explosion, two hundred and fifty people dead!

OCEANA:
See?

PIPELINE:
Mostly women and children.

OCEANA:
Life is cheap in Africa. Ha!

YOBE:
Unprecedented mass suicide.

PIPELINE:
Genocide.

YOBE:
And who's to blame but the people themselves?

PIPELINE:
Blame the victims?

YOBE:
Well, who is?

PIPELINE:
Or isn't.

YOBE:
But who cares, anyway? The oil pipelines are clearly marked "Restricted Area. Out of Bounds to all unauthorized persons." But no. They're blind. Deaf. What were they doing there, anyway?

OCEANA:
Praying! Chanting, "Jesus saves!" Ha! Ha! Ha! You tribespeople are a trip! Africa! Just look around you. Seen Rwanda? Somalia? Liberia? Sierra Leone? And now here, Sufferland? (*Chuckles.*) Well, now I understand the true spirit of the Organization of African Unity. Quite a great specimen of ritualized Organized Assassins' Union. The OAU. Ha! Ha! Ha! For a people so outstandingly endowed with . . . with passion, you know. That special brand of progress? Made in Africa, huh? Just one thing I know my Africans are doing right, at least. (*Mock laughter.*) Gentlemen, it's worth celebrating. Celebrate. Let's celebrate the organized animals' united genocide! It's the great tradition of being Born-Again-African . . . bloodbath. Drink! Drink to it! Africa's success stories. (*Toasting.*) To Africa's united planned progress in genocide! Ha! Ha! Ha!
(*His partners stare at each other. Silence.*)
Why look so morose? Is it not true? Friends, I'm proposing a well-deserved toast to your people. Let's drink.

PIPELINE:
(*Pushing his game.*) Play.
(*Reluctantly, they respond to the toast.*)

OCEANA:
Yes. Let's keep on playing. (*Back to the game.*)

YOBE:
Will they ever learn?

PIPELINE:
Who?

OCEANA:
Your people.

YOBE:
Black . . .

OCEANA:

It's in the blood . . . in the blood . . . (*Sighs, stretches.*) Scary, isn't it? Well, we need security reinforcement. I've sent for more.

PIPELINE:

For whom?

OCEANA:

My people, of course!

PIPELINE:

I hear you.

OCEANA:

We need more security guards.

PIPELINE:

But you have so many guards already.

OCEANA:

One can't be too safe. Not anymore.

PIPELINE:

Our people don't joke with their land. To them, Land *is* Life.

YOBE:

Perhaps, one can't blame them. What is a man worth without land, anyway?

OCEANA:

Stocks! (*Mock laughter.*)

YOBE:

Not for these people. They'll kill on sight anyone they think's an enemy.

OCEANA:

I know now why my British predecessors called this "the city of blood."

YOBE:

(*Interrupting.*) But they too killed millions.

PIPELINE:

Took millions . . .

OCEANA:

(*Laughing.*) And the summary again? Life is cheap in Africa! (*He breaks into mock laughter as he pushes his own game forward.*) But I know how to deal with anyone who crosses my line. (*Turning to* OMI, *who has just walked in with his shaving kit.*) Hear that, my sweet Papaya?
(*She nods her approval, goes behind him, and teases him with the blade as if beheading him.*)

OMI:

You asked for it. Are you now ready to be shaved?

OCEANA:

> (*Runs his fingers through his hair.*) Unruly stuff. Huh? I just can't wait.

OMI:

> Ready then? (*She starts to sharpen the blade.* OCEANA *turns to examine the blade.*)

OCEANA:

> Not sharp enough yet?

OMI:

> I've told you . . . Just wait and see. (*She starts to sharpen the blade as* OCEANA *observes the shaver with obvious discomfort. He checks the blade again.*)

OCEANA:

> Too sharp!. You're butcher or what?

PIPELINE:

> Want to kill the man?

OMI:

> (*Loud laughter.*) Won't be the first. (*Calmly to* OCEANA.) You're afraid?

OCEANA:

> Of course not! But see that blade you have looks too sharp. Scares the shit out of me . . . any man . . . (*To the men.*) Gentlemen, please check this.

PIPELINE:

> (*Inspecting the blade.*) Seems right to me, my friend.

OCEANA:

> True?

YOBE:

> You bet your life on it.

OCEANA:

> (*Laughing.*) Yours too. Life's too precious, my friend.

PIPELINE:

> For all of us!

YOBE:

> Absolutely!

OCEANA:

> (*Looks at his watch.*) Let's hear the news.

(OCEANA *presses the remote control. The screen shows the mob, protesting and chanting antigovernment slogans in a nonviolent demonstration in the streets. In silence, the men watch the action, while* OMI, *who seems absorbed*

*in the chants, sings along with the mob: Ozugo-o! Ozugo! Hell. Hell. Shell go-
go! Hell-Shell go go-o! Mob-Mobil. Mobilize-Mob! Mobilize Mob! Commot.
Hell. Shell go-goooooo!)*

OCEANA:
> (*Pulling her onto his lap.*) Babe, tell me. What are they saying?

OMI:
> Listen. I'll show you. (*Swinging her hips provocatively.*)

OCEANA:
> (*Teasing.*) Bad girl! Can't depend on you. No use. (*Meanwhile, the peo-
> ple's drumbeats intensify as OMI turns up the volume and entertains
> them with her modern dance movements. Amused, OCEANA mutters
> "Rascal! Such a rascal!" Then he turns away from her to the men.*) My
> friend, tell me, what the hell are they singing?

PIPELINE:
> Shell!

OCEANA:
> What?

PIPELINE:
> That Shell must go.

OCEANA:
> Nonsense! These idle people! Won't they go find some job?

PIPELINE:
> (*Pushing his own game.*) Where?

YOBE:
> (*Playing.*) Haven't we tried enough?

OCEANA:
> Precisely! We've tried everything to help them.

PIPELINE:
> They're not satisfied.

OCEANA:
> Until they begin to drink with our skulls?

PIPELINE:
> Well, they just want more.
> (*Nudging OCEANA to play, but his eyes are now glued to OMI, who's still
> absorbed in her dance.*)

OCEANA:
> (*Realizing himself.*) Ah. Are *your* people ever satisfied?

YOBE:
> Depends.

OCEANA:

>(*Still distracted.*) On who?

PIPELINE:

>(*Pushing his own game.*) You . . . Your turn, Director!
>(*But OCEANA is lost in thought.*)

YOBE:

>(*Nudging OCEANA, harder.*) We're waiting. Play!

OCEANA:

>Oh, can't you see? Keeps me busy . . .
>(*OMI stops dancing, falls into Oceana's arms.*)

PIPELINE:

>And forgetful?

YOBE:

>(*Laughing.*) Messed up?

OCEANA:

>(*Applauding her.*) Great, girl! Sure know how to turn a man's head!
>(*She stands behind OCEANA and places the shaver on the nape of his neck. OCEANA jumps.*)
>Ouch!

OMI:

>(*Still laughing.*) Jumping from a common blade? Our master is a coward.

OCEANA:

>You blame me? I love my life.

OMI:

>Who doesn't?

OCEANA:

>Well . . . (*Changes his mind, pulls his head away.*) You know, girl. I don't really think I'm ready for this now.

OMI:

>Later then?

OCEANA:

>Yes. These gentlemen are here for business.

OMI:

>(*Packing up the shaving kit.*) Good-bye then.

OCEANA:

>Are you leaving me?

OMI:

> Oh, no. As sure as death. Don't worry. I'll be back to take care of you!
> (*Chuckles.*)

OCEANA:

> That's my sweet . . .

(*He's silenced with a kiss from her. OMI tunes into a music station on the radio, then starts to leave. She's consciously, provocatively swinging her backside as he lustfully stares at her.*)

OCEANA:

> (*Shaking his head.*) A riot, that girl.

PIPELINE & YOBE:

> She is!

(*OMI steps aside with a loaded bag that she now clutches to her chest. Their hawkish eyes trail her steady strides up to the gate until lights fade out on her and the visitors take their leave of OCEANA. The screen is still on. OCEANA stands alone, watching the protesting mob with their drumbeats: "We want jobs! We want food! We want homes! Shell must go! Agip must go! Chevron must go! Texaco must go! Agip must go! Mobil must go! Willbros! Killbros-Willbros must go! Pollution! Pollution must go! Leave! Leave our oil! Leave! Leave our land! Oil! Oil! We have the oil! We want our oil! Oil! Oil! Oil! We want our land! Resource! Resource! Resource Control! Resource! Resource! Resource Control!" For a moment the protests continue. They're mixed with voices of the angry mob, shoving, quarreling among themselves, until one loud voice shouts, "Unite! Fight the enemy and not yourselves!" This is followed with rowdy questions: "Who? Who? Who's the enemy? Show me the enemy! Show me the enemy!" Someone points to the Oil Club: "There! There!" Suddenly, everyone else takes up the tune which soon grows into a choral chant of "There! There! There is our enemy! There! There! There is the enemy! There is the enemy!" The crowd gets more agitated, amplified by the chants into a marching tune. At first, their voices and chants are discordant, but as they begin to march and face the direction of the GRA/Oil Club they find harmony, and the tempo rises until they move, surging forward in angry uproar toward the exclusive villa.*)

MOVEMENT TWO

(Like many other villagers, hunting for food, water, and other essential commodities, OMI and IMO have joined the crowd of waiting hustlers gathering to buy fuel and kerosene at the barred Fuel/Petrol station in the Market-Square. As the long waiting and chattering continues, OMI displays some of the toilet rolls, soaps, and other household items she's taken from the villa, and now shares them with her friend.)

OMI:

(*Sharing the goods.*) I'm back. See?

IMO:

Trouble . . .

OMI:

Call me lucky.

IMO:

OK, Lucky Trouble! (*They laugh.*)

OMI:

I told you I wasn't born to suffer. My mother says to me always; "if you don't see how to do it, then do as you see it."

IMO:

Hmm . . . As they say "if you can't beat them, join them." (*Pause.*) Lucky your mother's there to teach . . . You know my story. (*Tearfully.*) They killed . . . killed my father for this oil . . . And . . . and then, my mother? Gone. Gone!

OMI:

(*Cuddling.*) I know. So painful your mother, too, became a victim of that oil pipeline blast . . .

IMO:

Poor mother. Just died like that. And to know that she joined the oil poachers, just minutes before that girl brought the lantern? And then the explosion! Mother had got nothing. Nothing! Not even a drop of fuel.

But she was cooked . . . fried . . . fried in that sizzling . . . Aaaah . . . (*Sobs.*)

OMI:

Don't cry, my dear. I feel your pain. We all do. But we can't change that now. What has happened has happened and we will now have to look to the future. It will never happen again. Never! We won't let them!

IMO:

But my parents are gone.

OMI:

Well . . . Not really. Your parents are resting in the arms of their creator. And they hear you . . . us now. (*Pause.*) You think they're sleeping? No! I believe they're all here . . . all our people slaughtered and butchered for asking to get a bite, just a slice of what belongs to them. No, dear. Our dead do not sleep. Neither will our God. So cheer up. Have faith. Resource control. That's all we ask and yet they won't let us. They shoot and kill us.

IMO:

So terrible! Took so many precious lives . . . (*Stops.*) And that greedy uncle who could have saved this whole community? Where was he? Where?

OMI:

Don't mind the yeye Chief. He thinks we don't know what he's doing with those thieves? We'll make them pay. All of them.

IMO:

Careful, though. Those people are callous.

OMI:

I know. (*Excitedly dangling a bunch of keys.*) Guess what? I got the key to . . .

IMO:

To his heart!

OMI:

Much like it. You know, I can enter anywhere in that villa.

IMO:

He gave them to you?

OMI:

How can? They're so shrewd, those people. Make you turn in every key to them as you leave everyday. My response? I made myself copies. They really think we're fools. (*Pause.*) Well, we'll keep playing the fool to get what we want. Ha! They'll see! Just who's fooling whom? (*They chuckle.*)

IMO:

The day they'll catch you? Hmm . . . They'll tear you open like they did those poor Odi-Choba women. They'll make you sweat.

OMI:

In my anus. Ha! Ha! Ha!

IMO:

Just that? They'll tear . . . rip you apart. Rape you right before your mother.

OMI:

Then rape my mother too and force me to watch.

IMO:

Ahaa! We all know. They think they'll always do what they like and get away?

OMI:

No way! Never again. And that's why we must deal with them.

IMO:

(*Chuckling.*) By stealing their soap and toilet paper? Well, they have too much. They won't even notice.

OMI:

Until they've been shaved clean. (*Pause.*) Have you seen Ikpoba yet?

IMO:

(*Saluting.*) To lick him hot? Razor-girl! Ride on!

OMI:

(*Strutting.*) I'm Naija-Hot, you know? You think they call me that for nothing?

IMO:

That I see. Go ahead. Shave all the men clean.

OMI:

But not my Ikpoba. I want him. (*Pause.*) Have you seen him?

IMO:

No. That boy has so licked the fire into you that your bottom sweats, just to lose sight of him for one minute.

OMI:

Say what you like. I love him. I need him to travel with.

IMO:

Your handbag? We know.

OMI:

Any girl who sees a guy as her handbag knows she'll end up empty-handed.

IMO:

And you're not?

OMI:

(*Gyrating.*) Girl, I need him. Want him so bad now. (*Turns to go.*)

IMO:

But can't you wait for fuel?

OMI:

I already gave the can to my mother. Ikpoba's all I need now. (*Departing.*) I'll go check up on him at his security post.

IMO:

So he got the job?

OMI:

Of course! What did you think?

IMO:

That anyone, even the director can easily smell the love oozing from both . . .

OMI:

Too bad for him. He can do anything, whatever. But he can't hide the sun. Can he?

IMO:

No. Haven't I told you what they did to me? That man?

OMI:

(*Soothing her.*) Who?

IMO:

That one who calls himself my uncle . . . the Chief . . . (*Showing her masked face with scars.*) See what they've done?

OMI:

The Chief? I know. Greed.

IMO:

Those white directors are even more terrible. They just have too much power and think they're clever.

OMI:

Yes. Until they cross me. (*Pulling her.*) Come.

IMO:

Tell me how you did it.

OMI:

What? With Ikpoba or Oceana?

IMO:

Well, both. You know . . . How come Oceana hired him as his personal guard?

OMI:

(*Swings her hips provocatively.*) He thinks he'll take me for nothing? (*They laugh.*) He tells me that he loves me. That he'll do whatever he can to please me. So I set a trap for him. Pushed Ikpoba on to him to give him a job. At first, he refused. Said he didn't like or trust the boy. That in any case, he'll need to consult first with Yobe and Pipeline, the Chief.

IMO:

Those crooks!

OMI:

Well, I quietly stayed away for days.

IMO:

Then he got itchy!

OMI:

And hungry. No one needed to tell him where to find the food. He sent for me, asked to see my brother. And Ikpoba got hired!

IMO:

(*Laughing.*) With you! Bad girl! Now I see how you both got the job! Spider! Spinning your webs all round! (*OMI does some gyrating, with IMO joining.*)

OMI:

Do we have a choice? We've got to survive.

IMO:

But how? See what they're doing to us. What are we going to do?

OMI:

With these people?

IMO:

Who else? Our lives depend on them.

OMI:

No. You mean *their* lives depend on us?

IMO:

Oh, well . . . If only they'll try to be honest and accept the truth for once.

OMI:

(*Seriously.*) Look, my friend. I've told you the best way for us to deal with these people is to do something. Something shocking. Terrible . . .

IMO:

Like killing them?

OMI:

Well, that too. But it's no use, killing.

IMO:

There's too much of that already.

OMI:

So what do we do?

IMO:

We need . . . need . . . to try something . . . something new (*Pause.*) Like kidnapping?

OMI:

(*Lighting up.*) Yes! The Director; that gang leader of the oil club!

IMO:

(*Excitedly.*) Great! Wonderful! Always full of ideas! (*Hugs OMI.*) That's why you'll be my friend forever. Yes! We'll teach them a lesson.

OMI:

Bring national . . .

IMO:

And international attention to our cause!

OMI:

That's it! That's when they'll start to pay attention to us and our needs.

IMO:

Isn't it sad?

OMI:

Well, if that's the only way they hear, we'll use any means to reach them.

IMO:

And then the press . . . media?

OMI:

Those too! They'll have a feast. Blow it to the roof top. Chant it night and day.

(*Play-acting. "This is the Sufferland Breaking News! American Oil Director kidnapped by village women! Leaders of the oil club abducted by rural women and youths! Manhunt is now under way to find them. And the kidnappers have named their ransom: Three billion! We'll keep you informed about any developments!" The play-acting ends. The girls burst into laughter.*)

OMI:

What a life where only the violent and tragic make news!

IMO:

We'll share this with our people when we meet.

OMI:

I must find Ikpoba now. Absolutely important that he stays on our side.

IMO:

Does he have any other choice?

OMI:

Well, who knows with these men?
(*They laugh. OMI starts leaving with the lights following her until they fade into the next stage.*)

MOVEMENT THREE

(IMO has joined the hustling and chattering of the mob behind the barricade leading to the fuel pump. They're pushing, shoving, and cursing one another as everyone struggles to edge their way into the crowded space near the pump/hose. IMO pushes her way through the chaotic line, goes over, pumps, and plays with the empty fuel hose. A male voice shouts: "Yes, sistah. Pump am! Pump am well-well! I dey your side!" Then another male replies: "Girl, pump it! Pump it to me! Give it to me! I'm ready!" The tense air breaks loose, as the starving community now rocks with laughter.)

IMO:
Are they selling?

CROSS RIVER:
Tomorrow.

IMO:
Then why wait? What for?

CROSS RIVER:
Tomorrow. Patience, my pickin.

IMO:
Patience? I'm tired! So tired, Anti. How long must we have to wait?

OSHIMI:
A good question!

(Laughter. They see IKPOBA/FUEL ATTENDANT approaching with the armed YOBE/POLICE OFFICER ONE and quickly resume their struggle for space in the line, with the cursing and pushing intensifying. Like generals inspecting an army, IKPOBA/FUEL ATTENDANT, with YOBE/POLICE OFFICER ONE behind him, now struts in front of them to show off the dry hose. He pumps out empty air, then blares out: "See? No fuel! No Kerosene! Go away!" But the people know better; they defy his order and trade more words and banter.)

OSHIMI:
You know when they do that?

CROSS RIVER:
Means there's fuel.

IMO:
Scare tactics, always.

OSHIMI:
That's the spirit. They think they're clever? Can you catch an old hen with mere chaff?

CROSS RIVER:
(*Teasing.*) Old layers like you should know better! (*They laugh.*)

OSHIMI:
And you? A spring chicken at 50, eh? Ha! What about those who can't do anything since they can't even find one short pump or limp hose? (*Laughter.*)

CROSS RIVER:
Tell me about that!

IMO:
Well, Anti, we plead guilty; some of us. And those of us who got laid . . .

OSHIMI:
Poor child! So you teachers have also joined the tribe of the unemployed, eh?

IMO:
Anti, na so we see-am-o!

OSHIMI:
But why? So who takes all that oil money? And who'll teach the children?

CROSS RIVER:
Vultures!

OSHIMI:
Both local and foreign breed. (*The women laugh.*)

CROSS RIVER:
See? See them hovering in the land?

IMO:
What do they care?

WOMEN:
Yes, what do they care?

OSHIMI:
Except for their own mouths and bellies. "Dem-dem," only.

CROSS RIVER:
And is that why they should lay off half the workers just because they say they want more profit and can't pay all that salary?

IMO:
And did you hear how much the so-called leaders spent globe-trotting and renovating their mansions in the state capital?

WOMEN:
No. Tell us.

IMO:
Billions!

WOMEN:
(*Alarmed.*) Eh?

IMO:
Enough to feed this nation for centuries!

OSHIMI:
And here we are.

CROSS RIVER:
Begging.

IMO:
Just to be able to survive.

WOMEN:
One day? Just one more day! (*Pause.*)

IMO:
And look around you. See? They're not even killing us alone. The trees too!

OSHIMI:
Our farmlands!

CROSS RIVER:
And rivers!

OSHIMI:
The environment.

CROSS RIVER:
Pollution!

OSHIMI:
Polluting the land, the rivers, our entire environment . . .

WOMEN:
All polluted.

IMO:
You said it.

OSHIMI:
Then she said it.

IMO:
They've killed everything with their oil pollution and spillage. We cannot breathe clean air. Fishes die or get fried in the polluted simmering rivers. Water—water everywhere. But we have no clean water to drink! And now we lose the land too?

OSHIMI:
No firewood because the plants and trees are soaked in oil. What do they expect us to cook with?

CROSS RIVER:
Your arms and legs!

OSHIMI:
Our men's runt sticks! (*Again the women break into laughter.*) My sisters. I'm not leaving here until I get what I need.

IMO:
Yes, mothers. We must stand up for our . . .

BONNY/OLD MAN:
(*Joining them.*) Rights in this country. Yes. You're not alone, my sisters! Guess how long I've been waiting here? Since yesterday.

IMO:
(*Alarmed.*) You mean you had to sleep here?

BONNY/OLD MAN:
What else? No water. No food . . .

IMO:
And sleep?

WOMEN:
Tomorrow! (*They all laugh. They spot some shady movements behind.*)

BONNY/OLD MAN:
I smell something fi . . . fishy . . .

IMO:
Fuel! It's there. (*Pause.*) Always deceiving us. Send us away so they can sell at bloated prices to their friends loaded with . . .

OSHIMI:
(*Still laughing and moving forward.*) They're not fooling me. I'm going to wait here till I get what I want!

CROSS RIVER:
(*Pushes forward.*) Me too!

OSHIMI:
These people think we're fools.

IMO:
No more!

(*Sound of a big Mercedes Benz car is heard, with honking in the background. PIPELINE/BUSINESSMAN emerges in flowing "agbada". He walks majestically past the crowd, pulls IKPOBA/FUEL ATTENDANT aside to whisper to him, after which he pushes some currency notes into the Attendant's cupped hand. The women are watching.*)

CROSS RIVER:
You see? Watch them. What did I tell you?

OSHIMI:
Bribery. It's there.

IMO:
Always. And they like to hoard and hoard everything.

OSHIMI:
For people wey get money.

IKPOBA/FUEL ATTENDANT:
(*Aside to PIPELINE/BUSINESSMAN.*) Oga, I hear. Make dem commot first.

PIPELINE/BUSINESSMAN:
I will come back later then?

IKPOBA/FUEL ATTENDANT:
Yes saar. Dem too plenty now.

PIPELINE/BUSINESSMAN:
Later then.
(*He walks towards the marketplace and watches the crowd from that distance.*)

IKPOBA/FUEL ATTENDANT:
(*To the crowd.*) You no see the sign? "*No Fuel.*" Go away!
(*IKPOBA/FUEL ATTENDANT is irritated and brandishes a sign as YOBE/POLICE OFFICER ONE follows with a whip. They push the crowd backwards. The crowd resists, resumes the banter.*)

OSHIMI:

Dis pickin. No push me-o! Na ordinary kalozin me I wan buy-o! I get motor?

CROSS RIVER:

(*Teasing.*) Who dash monkey banana?

OSHIMI:

My sister! Who dash monkey? We no kuku get motor.

CROSS RIVER:

Na common "kalozin" we wan buy.

OSHIMI:

Na we money too! Dem "shakara don too much."
(*Now angry, IKPOBA/FUEL ATTENDANT yanks and pushes them back. OSHIMI falls down, groaning, but other women help to lift her up again.*)

CROSS RIVER:

Boy, wetin? You wan kill de poor woman for common petrol?

IKPOBA/FUEL ATTENDANT:

So petrol dey common, abi? Why you dey trouble me for am now?

CROSS RIVER:

I beg, go siddon, o'jare! No kill we-o!

IMO:

(*Still nursing Oshimi's bruises.*) Your "shakara" don too much, sef. After all, na ordinary "Boy-Boy" you dey do!

IKPOBA/FUEL ATTENDANT:

(*Incensed, gives them a violent push.*) Me? Houseboy? I go teach you lesson-o!

IMO:

Go ahead. Let's see . . .

(*Vexed, he starts pulling off his shirt for a fight. Some of them start jeering and cheering him. But the older women try to stop him and he retreats. YOBE/POLICE OFFICER ONE continues his beat in another direction.*)

IMO:

Old boy, go open de tin. Just pour your yeye tin and let me go.

IKPOBA/FUEL ATTENDANT:

(*To the women.*) You see now? So na my yeye tin now? (*Pushing them away.*) Oya, make una commot. Commot all of you! (*They resist.*)

OSHIMI:

(*Confronting him.*) If you touch me again? I go . . .
(*IKPOBA/FUEL ATTENDANT retreats, goes behind the fuel pump to produce a koboko-whip with which he turns to the crowd.*)

IMO:

(*Daring him.*) Ha! Ha! Ha! Touch am now? If fowl say piss no hard, make e piss am now? (*IKPOBA/FUEL ATTENDANT now aims directly at her.*)

IKPOBA/FUEL ATTENDANT:

(*Threatening.*) Me?

IMO:

Yes! Wetin? Wetin you be sef?

IKPOBA/FUEL ATTENDANT:

(*Facing IMO.*) You wan try me? I go show you-o!

IMO:

Show me wetin? Wetin you get sef wey dey puff your yeye head so?

IKPOBA/FUEL ATTENDANT:

No try me-o! Or you go see!

IMO:

Dare!
(*He tries to target IMO, but the women form a human shield around the girl and block him.*)

CROSS RIVER:

(*Threatening.*) Try de girl now? Touch am!

IMO:

Touch me wit dat your dead stick. Just go ahead. Strike any woman here with dat your stump and you go smell your head. You common . . .

OSHIMI:

Attendant!

IMO:

Who dash am? *Servant!*

CROSS RIVER:

No be you even get de petrol. Common houseboy.

IKPOBA/FUEL ATTENDANT:

Me? Me, houseboy? Don't push me!
(*Scuffle. The mob rushes for the pump. Struggling and calling out.*)
Police! Police! Somebody call me de police! Dem go loot am! Petrol! Petrol! Get de petrol . . .

PIPELINE/BUSINESSMAN:

(*Stepping forward.*) Who?

WOMEN:

(*Teasing.*) Oga, you no hear? E say make we get de petrol.
(*They rush behind and start pumping the hidden fuel.*)

IKPOBA/FUEL ATTENDANT:
(*Hysterical.*) Police! Police, oga. Call me de police. Dey wan kill me-o! My oga! Oga go kill me-o!
(*PIPELINE/BUSINESSMAN* pulls out a cell phone and calls. Soon, *YOBE/ POLICE OFFICER ONE* returns.)

YOBE/POLICE OFFICER ONE:
What the hell is going on here?

WOMEN:
Shell . . . pump . . .

YOBE/POLICE OFFICER ONE:
(*Trying to disperse them with his baton.*) What's the matter with you people?

WOMEN:
Petrol!

IKPOBA/FUEL ATTENDANT:
No petrol! You deaf?

YOBE/POLICE OFFICER ONE:
(*Pushing them.*) You hear him? Private property. Out! Out!

IKPOBA/FUEL ATTENDANT:
Officer, save me. Oga . . . save me from dis people. My oga go kill me if . . .

WOMEN:
Make he kill you den. Na (h)only we fit to die?

IKPOBA/FUEL ATTENDANT:
You hear dem, Officer?

YOBE/POLICE OFFICER ONE:
(*Dispersing the crowd.*) Clear! Clear out all of you.

(*Still, they resist. A tug of war, with stampede following as they break through and try to grab the fuel. HADEJA working as a Hawker/Seller has arrived and entered the struggle to get her share.*)

HADEJA:
(*Excitedly.*) Thank you Lord!

CROSS RIVER:
Of petrol.

OSHIMI:
And kalozin!

(*They laugh, continue the tug of war with IKPOBA/FUEL ATTENDANT and YOBE/POLICE OFFICER ONE. PIPELINE/BUSINESSMAN pulls the Police Offi-*

cer aside, bribes him. Immediately, YOBE/POLICE OFFICER ONE pulls out his gun and mounts a guard in front of the pump as IKPOBA/FUEL ATTENDANT and PIPELINE/BUSINESSMAN whisper. Then they both disappear behind the fuel pump.)

HADEJA:
You see? You see dem?

WOMEN:
Today na today!

(They surge forward, suddenly pushing YOBE/POLICE OFFICER ONE. The gun falls, and they all struggle for it. IMO grabs the gun, hands it over to HADEJA, who aims it at YOBE/POLICE OFFICER ONE while IMO charges at IKPOBA/FUEL ATTENDANT. Seeing that YOBE/POLICE OFFICER ONE is now completely overwhelmed and disoriented, PIPELINE/BUSINESSMAN, wielding his cell phone, starts calling for security reinforcement.)

PIPELINE/BUSINESSMAN:
Just wait for the mobile police.

WOMEN:
Who? Police? *(The women go into a mock drama of the policemen taking bribe.)* "Woman, wetin you carry? Open, woman! Show de tin wey you carry!" Make dem come! Come! Come!

(They cheer and jeer, rush at YOBE/POLICE OFFICER ONE and hold him down.)

IMO:
Come now. Ready.

YOBE/POLICE OFFICER ONE:
(Panting.) My . . . my . . . gun . . . You take my gun? Woman, you dey play with fire!

IMO:
I am fire!

CHORUS OF WOMEN:
Fire! Fire! We are fire!

OSHIMI:
(Calmly to IMO.) Careful, child.

IMO:
No! Not with these bastards!

CHORUS OF WOMEN:
Finish am!

IMO:

All of them!

CROSS RIVER:

Child, don't. Too much sacrifice.

OSHIMI:

We've lost too much already.

IMO:

Then let it be.

CHORUS OF WOMEN:

Show dem! Show dem!

OSHIMI:

There's nothing to show. Animals . . .

CROSS RIVER:

Dey play . . .

IMO:

With lions?

CHORUS OF WOMEN:

Yes, lion! We be lion!

OSHIMI:

Hungry!

CROSS RIVER:

And angry!

IMO:

Falling? What do I care? I'm down. Down already? So why should I fear?

CROSS RIVER:

(*Chuckling, calming her down.*) Your head, child.
(*She takes the weapon from her.*)

OSHIMI:

(*Teasing.*) Sure she's not lost it already?

CROSS RIVER:

We've lost too much already.

IMO:

And so?

CROSS RIVER:

It matters.

OSHIMI:

Nothing matters . . .

CROSS RIVER:
No. Not any more.

OSHIMI:
We get value?

IMO:
Oh, yes we do! That's why we must show them. Take control of our lives.

CHORUS OF WOMEN:
(*Drumming*) True, daughter. She said it! Show! Show! Show them! Women take control. Take control of our lives!

(*Suddenly, BONNY/POLICE OFFICER TWO arrives and fires tear-gas into the crowd. Smoke, commotion, as the people are choking and fleeing. HADEJA is arrested, handcuffed, and pushed into a corner. Meanwhile, IMO has broken away from the crowd and is yelling: "Attendant! Where's that attendant?" The crowd returns to join her. They find IKPOBA/FUEL ATTENDANT getting ready to dispense fuel to PIPELINE/BUSINESSMAN. IMO quickly moves, grabs a container, and insists on being served, with other women following and clamoring. "We wan kalozin. We wan fuel. Sell! Sell! Sell us fuel!"*)

IKPOBA/FUEL ATTENDANT:
Women. Trouble . . . trouble . . .
(*Desperate, he flings Imo's container away. She picks it up, returns, and replaces it.*)
You dey mad?

IMO:
You too. You're mad. Why? Why give fuel to him and not to us?

IKPOBA/FUEL ATTENDANT:
If you wan fuel, den pay . . . (*Showing.*) Dat na One Thousand. . . .

CHORUS OF WOMEN:
What?

IKPOBA/FUEL ATTENDANT:
Yes. Take it or leave it.

IMO:
Thief!

CHORUS OF WOMEN:
Tief! Olleh! Tief! Oshi! Barawo!

IMO:
Yes. That's how you people hike up everything.

OSHIMI:
So poor people no go get . . .

IMO:
You create artificial scarcity.

CHORUS OF WOMEN:
To cheat us.

CROSS RIVER:
My pickin! Poor wo . . . man no get broda!

IMO:
Yes, my people. Failure is an orphan.

IKPOBA/FUEL ATTENDANT:
Yes. You say you be sometin? Pay now. Time to show say you be sometin.

IMO:
Yes, I am. Somebody.

CHORUS OF WOMEN:
A teacher!

IKPOBA/FUEL ATTENDANT:
(*Mock laughter.*) So you be *teasha*? Ordinary teasha dey make all dis wahala since? Ha, teasha! Wetin you sabi? You empty pocket!

IMO:
Wretched thing!

IKPOBA/FUEL ATTENDANT:
(*Laughing.*) See you! See am! See who dey call person wretched. Government don pay you for so many months? You jobless . . .

IMO:
Is it your business?

IKPOBA/FUEL ATTENDANT:
(*Teasing, dancing.*) Ha, teasha. So-so gbese . . . debt . . . full here full dere. No wonder body dey pain you. Ha! Pepper-Eye! Hungry woman. Look him face. Monkey zoo. Na wetin do your face? Ohooo! Cockroach! Na cockroach lick him face.
(*He laughs and teases. IMO is now more incensed and confronts PIPELINE/BUSINESSMAN.*)

IMO:
It's people like you who turn this country upside down.

PIPELINE/BUSINESSMAN:
Woman, go away! I have no business with you.

IMO:

Oh, yes you do. Why must you bribe your way through everything?

PIPELINE/BUSINESSMAN:

(*Arrogantly.*) Am I in your way?

IMO:

Yes, you are! All of you, wrecking us with your ill-gotten wealth.

PIPELINE/BUSINESSMAN:

You are just jealous.

IMO:

Of you? For what?

CHORUS OF WOMEN:

(*Jeering and cheering.*) Yes! Tell am! Curse am!

PIPELINE/BUSINESSMAN:

Frustrated old maid! Go find yourself a husband!

IMO:

Certainly not your type!

PIPELINE/BUSINESSMAN:

What would I do with a thing like you?

IMO:

When the time comes you'd wish you had this *thing* like me.

PIPELINE/BUSINESSMAN:

Hear her? Your type? Never! Never have any dealing with your type, woman! You must be dreaming.

IMO:

And I'll wake up. Yes we must. Just wait. Time is . . .

PIPELINE/BUSINESSMAN:

(*Laughing.*) What time?

CHORUS OF WOMEN:

You'll see.

PIPELINE/BUSINESSMAN:

Ah, women! And time? Oh well, nothing new.

CHORUS OF WOMEN:

You'll see.

PIPELINE/BUSINESSMAN:

If you say so. (*Pause.*) But I know . . . We'll take it . . . whatever comes . . . We'll be ready.

IMO:

When judgment comes?

PIPELINE/BUSINESSMAN:
(*Laughing in her face.*) Dreamer! You wish!

CHORUS OF WOMEN:
Are you ready then? Repent! Repent! Jesus is coming back for him world!

PIPELINE/BUSINESSMAN:
These charlatans! Driving everyone crazy with their religious . . . antics. Nonsense! What's this country coming to? Won't let one sleep or rest. In traffic, marketplace, churches, stores, everywhere. Swarms of fleas buzzing in your ear. (*Parodying.*) "Repent! Repent! Change! Jesus saves! Jesus is coming! Repent!" Jesus is coming to where?

IMO:
(*Taunting him.*) Here, to get you. Make your dirty mouth bleed.
(*He yanks her. IMO falls, rises, and braces for a fight. The crowd continues cheering and jeering.*)

IKPOBA/FUEL ATTENDANT:
Do your worse now. (*Calls back BONNY/POLICE OFFICER TWO.*)

BONNY/POLICE OFFICER TWO:
(*Returning.*) Na wetin? Man no go rest? Leave me o'jare! I tire!

CHORUS OF WOMEN:
I tire no be lazy! Ha! Ha! Ha!
(*He steps behind. They rush into the station, overpower IKPOBA/FUEL ATTENDANT, and loot the fuel and kerosene.*)

PIPELINE/BUSINESSMAN:
Don't worry. I've called for more security reinforcement.

CHORUS OF WOMEN:
(*Laughing.*) Quick, quick, make you call dem. No to you start am?

PIPELINE/BUSINESSMAN:
(*Spiteful look at IMO.*): It's all her fault. That witch. You think you can get away with this?

IMO:
(*Threatening.*) Don't try me-o! (*YOBE/POLICE OFFICER ONE returns.*)

CHORUS OF WOMEN:
(*Shouting.*) Na Operation Sweep-o! Run! Run! (*Crowd flees.*)

PIPELINE/BUSINESSMAN:
(*To YOBE/POLICE OFFICER ONE.*) That's the criminal!

YOBE/POLICE OFFICER ONE:
(*Grabbing OSHIMI.*) This one?

PIPELINE/BUSINESSMAN:

No. De one behind wey him face be like Ekpo . . . mask. Miss Ugly . . . She started it all.

(*YOBE/POLICE OFFICER ONE makes a dash for IMO, who tries to flee.*)

YOBE/POLICE OFFICER ONE:

Halt!

IMO:

Why? What for?

YOBE/POLICE OFFICER ONE:

You've been arrested Under Section 10. Subsection 36458 of the Penal Code law.

IMO:

Nonsense!

YOBE/POLICE OFFICER ONE:

What? Me? Nonsense? (*He grabs her.*)

IMO:

Leave me alone. I'm innocent. That's the man you should arrest.

(*YOBE/POLICE OFFICER ONE slaps her. Her face is bleeding as she's being handcuffed.*)

PIPELINE/BUSINESSMAN:

(*Mocking IMO.*) You think this is a jungle? A lawless country where you can just run your filthy mouth anyhow? Well, now you know. This fucking country does have some law and order! Ha! Ha! Ha!

(*Exit PIPELINE/BUSINESSMAN. Sounds of his Mercedes blasting off. IMO kicks and curses as she is being dragged away. As soon as the Businessman leaves, the women start pleading for the girls in custody.*)

OSHIMI:

I beg. Make you lef am.

CROSS RIVER:

Na my friend pickin be dat.

BONNY/POLICE OFFICER TWO:

(*Ignoring them.*) And den?

OSHIMI:

I beg.

YOBE/POLICE OFFICER ONE:

Na beg-beg I go chop?

(*Aside, OSHIMI and CROSS RIVER confer and produce some roasted corn, which they offer to the police officers. Indignant, the police officers start walking away, but the women continue pleading.*)

BONNY/POLICE OFFICER TWO:

You mean say I be cheap article wey you fit buy wit . . . wit . . . nonsense . . . chaff? (*Mock laughter.*) Ha, country! Police don see somtin
for naija! Ha! Police don turn to article without value. (*Sternly.*) Look,
here woman. You see dis uniform? E be like wetin you fit buy wit . . .
wit . . . corn?

OSHIMI:

(*Pleading, adding some currency notes.*) I beg. Take. Na de only tin we
get to chop we give you so.

CROSS RIVER:

(*Passionately.*) I swear. God dey hear we. Na de only tin we get be dat.
I beg.

BONNY/POLICE OFFICER TWO:

So that is all?

OSHIMI AND CROSS RIVER:

Everything. All we get.
(*BONNY/POLICE OFFICER TWO stares at them briefly, then slowly leans
to take his prize.*)

YOBE/POLICE OFFICER ONE:

God knows I'm hungry too.

OSHIMI AND CROSS RIVER:

Like we dey too! Plenty plenty of we! Hunger! Hunger dey wire we
head!

BONNY/POLICE OFFICER TWO:

For three months, dem never pay us. (*OSHIMI is offering another corn
to YOBE/POLICE OFFICER ONE.*)

OSHIMI:

So de government expect you to work for empty stomach?

YOBE/POLICE OFFICER ONE:

Bring am, my sista. (*Takes the corn and eats greedily. BONNY/POLICE
OFFICER TWO is in his own corner, eating greedily too.*) Dem say "half
bread beta pass noting."

OSHIMI AND CROSS RIVER:

True-true, my broda! Half bread beta pass notin.

YOBE/POLICE OFFICER ONE:

(*Mouthful.*) Hmm . . . my sistah. Tell me how man for do! (*The police
officers join the women's laughter between mouthfuls of corn.*) Work-
work, no pay. How monkey go dey work, baboon go dey chop? Eh?

BONNY/POLICE OFFICER TWO:

And you hear de president? (*Parodying, play-acting.*) "Fellow Nai . . .
Sufferlands! Hard times ahead! So tighten your belt!" (*Laughter.*)

OSHIMI AND CROSS RIVER:
(*Mimicking.*) Even when E dey untie him own? (*More laughter.*)

YOBE/POLICE OFFICER ONE:
My sista. "Dat na special brand of Sufferland Justice."

OSHIMI AND CROSS RIVER:
Na so we see-am-o! (The police officers release their captives.)

BONNY/POLICE OFFICER TWO:
(*Bites deeply into the corn husk.*) And dis na my own special brand! Ha! Ha! Ha!

OSHIMI:
I beg, my broda. Don't forget dat we other small sistah.

YOBE/POLICE OFFICER ONE:
Dat one?

CROSS RIVER:
Yes-o, my broda. Make you forgive am.

BONNY/POLICE OFFICER TWO:
I see-am. E too make trouble.

OSHIMI:
Lef am. Na small pickin.

YOBE/POLICE OFFICER ONE:
E still dey wash him belle?
(*They laugh.*)

CHORUS OF WOMEN:
True-true! E no sabi anytin. I beg lef am for us.

BONNY/POLICE OFFICER TWO:
Ok ay-o! As you talk. Me I go tell de sergeant to lef am . . . say una don pay.

CHORUS OF WOMEN:
Our broda! Thank you-o!!!

YOBE/POLICE OFFICER ONE:
(*Studies the girl for a while. His partner releases her as he speaks.*) You self, you too make trouble. Proper *gba-gba-ti* girl you be! You too sabi. (*Sternly.*) Now look here. If you ever enter trouble again, I no go save you-o! Go now and behave yourself. Go home, woman! Your faith has saved you. No be so de church people dey talk am? Tomorrow is another day. (*He drinks, belches, and starts picking at his teeth.*) Me, I don belle full . . .

OSHIMI AND CROSS RIVER:
No. You belle-wise!

BONNY/POLICE OFFICER TWO:
Yes, my people. (*Emphatically.*) Belle-Wise! Wetin concern agbero wit overload? Ha! Ha! Ha! (*Belches, hiccups, loudly.*) Who say I never do my job? Country can go to blazes! Ha! Ha! Ha! Go home, women. The men and children are waiting.

OSHIMI:
For dem grave . . .

YOBE/POLICE OFFICER ONE:
Dem kill your own too? (*OSHIMI nods, sighs.*)

OSHIMI:
Yes. Just for dat protest.

CROSS RIVER:
And my own too.

BONNY/POLICE OFFICER TWO:
(*Somber.*) Bloody . . .

IMO:
Country.

YOBE/POLICE OFFICER ONE:
Waste. Bloody waste. (*Pensive.*) Just go and rest. Too risky here. (*He whistles, turns businesslike again, and starts walking as he hears loud bugle sounds from their distant headquarters.*)

CHORUS OF WOMEN:
(*Departing.*) Thank you! Thank you! Oga!

YOBE/POLICE OFFICER ONE:
No problem. I dey for your side. Poor man no get broda.

CHORUS OF WOMEN:
Yes, broda. Failure is an orphan.

BONNY/POLICE OFFICER TWO:
(*To the girls.*) You know where I am. Call me whenever you need me.

CHORUS OF WOMEN:
We will. Thank you. (*Exit Police Officers. Light dims. Everyone now hurries home.*)

MOVEMENT FOUR

(*Twilight. The Market-Square is empty except for IMO in combat attire. She crosses, pacing up and down between the marketplace and the locked GRA/Oil Club. She's talking to herself as she displays some protest literature not far from the gate of the GRA/Oil Club. HADEJA as the Hawker/Seller soon appears with her fruit basket [bananas, oranges, and paw-paw] delicately balanced on her head. She looks exhausted but graceful and dignified in her slow march to the GRA/Oil Club with her usual chants and erotic steps.*)

HADEJA:

Buy my orange! Buy banana! Sweet sweet paw-paw! (*No response. Her chanting gets more desperate.*) Buy my orange, banana, paw-paw-papaya! Na de sweetest juice in the world!

IMO:

(*Jokingly.*) Old girl, you no dey tire?

HADEJA:

Do I have a choice?

IMO:

Go home, my friend. Those people have more than enough juices to last them a time.

(*IMO improvises her new anthem or National Pledge, which she recites with HADEJA.*)

I pledge to Sufferland my country.

HADEJA:

To be faithful, loyal, and (ho)nest. To serve Sufferland with all my strength. To defend her unity and honor.

IMO:

(*Loudly.*) SOLD!

HADEJA:

Sold-Sold-Sold-Sold!

IMO:

So help me.

HADEJA:

God! And wish me . . .

IMO:

Luck. Amen! (*Pause.*) God save!

HADEJA:

Sufferland!!

(*IMO stands at attention, gives military salute, and resumes her new National Pledge. A sudden commotion—people running and being pursued by others. The runners are OMI and IKPOBA. OSHIMI and CROSS RIVER are in pursuit.*)

OSHIMI:

(*Desperately.*) Who dey dere? I beg. Holl-am! Holl-am for me!

CROSS RIVER:

I beg. My son. Come back.

(*The fugitives quicken their pace. OMI is dressed to kill in her short hot pants. IKPOBA, also known as the Bandit-Boy, is in his baggy trousers, T-shirt, and baseball cap.*)

OSHIMI:

(*Panting.*) Holl am!

HADEJA AND IMO:

Who?

OSHIMI:

De gal. My daughter. Lost.

(*OMI dribbles her as she pursues. OSHIMI misses a step, stumbles, and stops to catch her breath. CROSS RIVER assists her as she too cries out for help. The teenagers turn to romance and tease the women, who look helpless. IMO and HADEJA struggle to help the mothers block the way. But then voices of other youths are encouraging the fugitives with cheers.*)

OSHIMI:

Is there nobody ready to help a tired woman? Helepu! Helepu meeee-o!

OMI:

Don't touch me!

IKPOBA:

Don't touch me-o!

(*IKPOBA quickly pulls out a string from his pocket and, with OMI, ties it across the road to block their assailants. Meanwhile, IMO tries to restrain OSHIMI and CROSS RIVER from the chase.*)

OSHIMI:

Hollaaaaaam!!

VOICES OF YOUTHS:
Go. Ride on!

CHORUS OF WOMEN:
Stop, children! Children stop!

VOICES OF YOUTHS:
Don't stop! Keep moving! These parents!

CHORUS OF WOMEN:
Children!

VOICES OF YOUTHS:
These parents! Parents! Parents! What can they do anyway? What do they want?

CHORUS OF WOMEN:
Keep you out of trouble.

OMI:
But we *are* trouble.

IKPOBA:
Yes. So how can anyone keep us away from *us*?

VOICES OF YOUTHS:
Keep us prisoners at home.

CHORUS OF WOMEN:
Safety. Your safety!

VOICES OF YOUTHS:
Really? Can they afford it?

OMI AND IKPOBA:
Can they afford anything?

VOICES OF YOUTHS:
Our parents. Wretched wretched and poor.

OMI AND IKPOBA:
Tired, wretched . . .

VOICES OF YOUTHS:
(*Chanting.*) Poor . . . poorer . . . poorest! Go girl! We dig your style. We won't yield! No won't yield! We're following in your footsteps!
(*The youths break into rap music and dance, which the fugitive pair gladly lead as they swing, dance and hold onto each other seductively. The parents watch in absolute dismay.*)

CROSS RIVER:
(*Sighing.*) What is our world turning to?

OMI:
(*Smiling, flexing muscles.*) Youths!

IKPOBA AND OMI:

Yeah. Yeah! We got the power! More power to the youths!
(*They laugh.*)

OSHIMI:

(*To the women.*) My sistah. See me see trouble-o!

(*The women are in shock and remain silent. HADEJA exits in anger. OSHIMI takes out something from her bra. Then she approaches her daughter OMI. CROSS RIVER too takes out a similar thing from her own bra as she approaches the defiant couple.*)

CROSS RIVER:

Come. Come home.

IKPOBA:

Where is the home?

CROSS RIVER:

I know (*Choking.*) I know it's nothing but it's ours.

IKPOBA:

Then stay there. I won't (*Emphatically.*) I will not!
(*He swings and does an erotic jig with OMI.*)

OMI:

You mothers leave us alone to fend for ourselves. Can't you see we're ready to go?

OSHIMI:

(*Pleading with her daughter.*) Then take it, my daughter. Rich or poor, I want you alive; not dead.

OMI:

(*Curious.*) What is that?

OSHIMI:

You know. Raincoat.

CROSS RIVER:

(*Irritated.*) Condom. Not raincoat. Let's name it right. Call it what it is. These children need to get the point. Protection! Protection! Protection! (*The defiant pair laugh loud, with voices of the other youths magnifying their laughter.*)

IKPOBA AND OMI:

These parents must be running out of ideas. You think we know nothing?

CROSS RIVER:

And AIDS too is out there . . .

OSHIMI:
With unwanted babies calling!

CHORUS OF WOMEN:
(*Chanting.*) Oh, so many—so many many troubles calling our youths!

OSHIMI:
It's raining.

CROSS RIVER:
It's wet.

OSHIMI:
Slippery. Life's tough.

CROSS RIVER:
And rough.

CHORUS OF WOMEN:
Children you must arm yourselves with raincoats in the rainy . . .

CROSS RIVER:
Stormy weather.

IKPOBA AND OMI:
(*In a singsong manner.*) No, we won't!

CHORUS OF WOMEN:
Oh yes, you will!

OMI:
What for?

IKPOBA:
You know you're losing anyway.

OSHIMI:
But see, children? What you have, you hold!

CROSS RIVER:
Protect . . .

CHORUS OF WOMEN:
Protection! Protection! Protection!

IKPOBA AND OMI:
And you think we don't know?

OSHIMI:
Well, nobody says you don't.

CROSS RIVER:
And you think you know more than we do?

OSHIMI:
Yes. That's kids nowadays. They think they know more than their parents.

IKPOBA AND OMI:

>   (*Taunting.*) And we do? Doubt it?
>   (*Again, they swing and break into erotic dance-steps*).

IKPOBA:

>   You doubt it? That's where we're going.

OMI:

>   To the GRA/Oil Club!

IKPOBA:

>   To arm ourselves.

OMI:

>   By hook or crook.

OSHIMI:

>   And get killed?

CROSS RIVER:

>   Or jailed?

IKPOBA:

>   It doesn't matter.

OMI:

>   Nothing matters.

IKPOBA:

>   Anymore. (*Silence.*) And if we don't go? Can you feed . . .

OMI:

>   Fend for us?

IKPOBA:

>   Send us to school?

OMI:

>   Give us employment?

IKPOBA:

>   Buy our clothing?

OMI:

>   Provide all our needs?

IKPOBA:

>   So what choices have we got?

OMI:

>   But only to take destiny into our hands.
>   (*As they speak, the women watch helplessly.*)

CROSS RIVER:

>   (*Tearfully.*) Son, the "hell" people don't joke . . .

IKPOBA:
Shell!

CROSS RIVER:
Yes. They'll kill you . . . anybody in their way.

IKPOBA:
(*Beating his chest.*) Let them try!

CROSS RIVER:
You know they will.

IKPOBA:
Then it's my lot.

OSHIMI:
No, it's not. You're taking the law into your own hands.

OMI:
So?

IKPOBA:
It's her life.

OMI:
(*Strutting.*) It's my life.

OSHIMI:
Then take it.

CROSS RIVER:
They'll kill you.

OMI:
Whatever. I'm going!

IKPOBA:
To teach those bas . . .

(*Swiftly, he grabs OMI. With the voices of youths still cheering and blast-ing the air with their rap music even louder, the rebellious pair does some final erotic dance-steps together and run toward the gate of the GRA/OIL Club. For a while after their departure, the women stare helplessly at one another, until OSHIMI breaks into a somber tune, which the other women join.*)

CROSS RIVER:
(*Subdued.*) Sad.

OSHIMI:
Very sad. What can we do?

IMO:
Something's got to be done.

OSHIMI:
How?

CROSS RIVER:
(*Voice cracking.*) How . . . ? Sisters, we're losing.

IMO:
And violated! Didn't I tell you about my own experience? (*Sobs.*) They ate me . . . raw . . . (*Sobbing.*)

OSHIMI:
Yes. Losing on all sides.

CROSS RIVER:
Losing our sons.

OSHIMI:
Our daughters.

CROSS RIVER:
Losing brothers . . . sisters.

CHORUS OF WOMEN:
Losing! Losing! Losing . . . on all sides . . . Everything.

IMO:
Mothers, we've got to do something! Something.

OSHIMI:
She's said it. Said it!

CROSS RIVER:
She's said it!
(*They stretch their hands, link up, and spread across the road. Now the women have formed a human shield across the road in the marketplace.*)

IMO:
From now on, nobody goes through the marketplace without us.

CROSS RIVER:
(*Firmly.*) From now on, nobody passes any road without us.

IMO:
We are together.

CHORUS OF WOMEN:
Together! Together! Together! Women stay together!

IMO:
(*Excitedly calling.*) Mothers!

CHORUS OF WOMEN:
Eeeeh!

IMO:
Who owns this land?

CHORUS OF WOMEN:
We own this land!

IMO:
Who spoils this land?

CHORUS OF WOMEN:
We spoil this land.

IMO:
Who sweeps this land?

CHORUS OF WOMEN:
We sweep the land!

IMO:
Who seals this land?

CHORUS OF WOMEN:
We seal the land.

IMO:
Who heals the wounds?

CHORUS OF WOMEN:
We . . .
(*They are still madly absorbed in this incantatory chant when* HADEJA *as Hawker/Seller returns wailing as she runs back from the GRA/OIL Club gate.*)

OSHIMI:
Oh, I'm dead, my daughter! (*Chasing* HADEJA.)

CHORUS OF WOMEN:
Another daughter.

OSHIMI:
(*Pleading.*) Tell me what is wrong? What did they do to you?
(HADEJA *ignores her mother and continues hastily and tearfully on her journey home.*)
Somebody help! Help! That's the only one I have left. And now I'm losing her too? (*The women try to stop* HADEJA, *but she pushes her way through and marches on.*)

HADEJA:
Leave me alone, everybody, I'm tired. Tired, I too am ready now to find my own way!

IMO:
(*Thrusts herself on the road to block* HADEJA.) Come with me. Where is the fruit?
(HADEJA *sobs.*)

Gone? They took it? (*HADEJA nods.*) Ah, I know they do. You too, raped? (*Silence.*)

OSHIMI:

(*Hysterical.*) Whooooooooo? Who dares touch my daughter?

CROSS RIVER:

Who dares-who dares! Daughter of the land—daughter of the sea!

IMO:

They did it—did it. Yes they did! (*More sobbing from HADEJA.*)

CROSS RIVER:

The soldiers?

(*At this point, HADEJA explodes into tears. The women encircle her as she weeps silently. But with each question, she nods her head.*)

CHORUS OF WOMEN:

(*Stunned.*) Soldiers? Police?

OSHIMI:

(*Choking with tears.*) B . . . bu . . . they were sent here to pro . . . tect us?

CROSS RIVER:

You think it matters to them?

OSHIMI:

Is it the White man? (*Silence.*)

CROSS RIVER:

The Government Official?

IMO:

Or the Chief?

(*HADEJA weeps louder. IMO comforts her.*)

HADEJA:

(*Tearfully.*) All . . . all of them. Cut deep with their knife. I fought. Tried . . . tried to close my eyes. Tight. (*Screams.*) Aaah! How I prayed God to close them forever. Bury me, alive. But when I opened, I saw him . . . grinning . . . grinning into my face. The Thief . . . (*Screams.*) Aaaaaah! God, now I know . . . You? Man? Why did you do this to me? Why? True? God? (*Singsong.*) What . . . what are you? Where? Where are you? (*The women hold her as she falls.*)

OSHIMI:

Child. Know you're not alone. (*HADEJA breaks away from the women but IMO persists.*)

OSHIMI:

(*Frustrated.*) Are they never tired of ruining . . . ?

IMO:

> Killing us!

CROSS RIVER:

> At Odi?

CHORUS OF WOMEN:

> They raped and killed women!

OSHIMI:

> In Choba?

CHORUS OF WOMEN:

> They raped and killed women!

CROSS RIVER:

> Across the sea?

CHORUS OF WOMEN:

> They raped and killed women.

OSHIMI:

> In the land?

CHORUS OF WOMEN:

> They raped . . . tore up . . . aaaaaaah!

CROSS RIVER:

> And still . . .

CHORUS OF WOMEN:

> They're raping, selling, and killing us.

HADEJA:

> (*Exploding.*) Mother, I tell you. I won't go there anymore. But you keep pushing, pushing me to go . . .

OSHIMI:

> To sell. Yes. It's my fault. But child, what could I do? We had nothing. Nothing to eat.

HADEJA:

> But you let her, your daughter Omi run to those foreigners . . .

OSHIMI:

> She is selling too, daughter. She says she has to sell . . . what she has.

HADEJA:

> (*Stripping her clothes.*) Am I the one to be left out? I too have to sell what I got. See? Mother, see? I'm tired. I too can sell. (*She gets hysterical, dances provocatively.*) And sell I will! It's easier, much easier if you let me go? What more have you got to lose?

OSHIMI:

> (*Holding her.*) You, my daughter!

HADEJA:

(*Laughing.*) I too have got to go.

OSHIMI:

Daughter, do it for me. Please!

HADEJA:

I said I won't. Now, I too I'm going. Yes. As they say, if you can't beat them, join them! (*Pause.*) Five years out of school. Robbed of life. Robbed of dignity. And what have I become? A petty trader. Yes. That's all. Is that all I should be about? Is it? No. I know I'm worth more. Much more than they're willing to buy or pay for. And now I say no. I too am fixing my own price. (*Deliberately.*) I am going to Europe . . . to Italy where the business is hot . . . and I too will sell like hot cakes. He said it, the great Thief . . . I mean the Chief, our leader. (*Strutting.*) Yes, I'm gonna cash in on my own luck. (*IMO follows and pleads with HADEJA, pulls her aside.*)

IMO:

Don't. Don't go. Let's stay here. Work it out together in our home . . .

HADEJA:

This is no home.

IMO:

But it is ours.

HADEJA:

Yes, ours. Taken. Taken! The nation? Prostitutes . . . Look, if this is our land, who rules it? (*Screams.*) Foreigners! Strangers! Who controls it? Do we have a voice? Do we? How can we be in our own homes and be so afraid? Are we not the strangers . . . strangers in our own land? (*Pause.*) Now hear this. (*She quickly pulls out the admission offers she received from the University, and reads.*)

> From:
> Director of Undergraduate Admissions
> National University
> Naija State
> Suffferland
> November 20, 1997.
>
> Dear Ms. Hadeja Atiene,
> It's with great pleasure that I offer you admission to the Department of Law in this great citadel of learning. In accepting this offer, you will be joining students and staff with world renowned potentials and

credentials. The deadline for you to secure your admission is December 1, 1997. To ensure your place, you must deposit a nonrefundable fee of 10,000.00 Naija cash to the university Bursar. Thereafter, you are expected to report for orientation and classes on December 8, at 9 A.M. at our Pipeline Campus auditorium. We look forward to your participation in our rich, rigorous campus life.

Congratulations!

Signed,

Professor Future Prospect,

Registrar of National University, Sufferland.

(*After reading the letter aloud,* HADEJA *holds it up, shouts to the women.*)

HADEJA:

And mother, what is today's date? Ha! Years after, after my deadline and I'm still here. Searching . . . Searching for the deposit to . . . to . . . my life. Yes. (*Shakes her buttocks vigorously.*) Here it is. My insurance for tomorrow. Ha! Ha! Ha!.

(*Laughing, she steps towards her mother, tears the letter right in her mother's face, and throws it into the air like confetti.*)

There goes the dream! For one . . . two . . . three . . . four . . . five years . . . Five good years of my youth, I struggled, studied, and suffered to get admitted into the university. What use is it now? What use? (*Hysterical.*) All those thousands and millions of educated youth who struggled to gain the education and find jobs? Where are they now? Where are the jobs? Where are the youths? On the streets! In graves or jails! Mother, I too am tired. I'm taking the easy way out. I'm joining my sister. Yes, Omi! She tells me the foreigner is taking her to Italy, America, or some other European city. I too am going! (*She turns her back, starts running.*)

IMO:

(*Chasing.*) The West. Weird place! Don't go. No! Oh no, please! Don't. In the name of everything you cherish. Don't! They'll ruin you there. They'll wreck you, turn you to prost . . .

HADEJA:

Yes, make money. Cash. Hard, hard, currency. That is what speaks.

IMO:

(*Desperate.*) Bloody. They'll get a dog to . . . to . . . Oh no, don't you see? Look at me. My own uncle gave me to the foreigner who gave me to . . . to . . . His dog? (*Screams.*) Aya ya ya yaaaah! (CROSS RIVER *steps in and holds* IMO *back, knowing how emotional she can get when she speaks about her own experience.*)

CROSS RIVER:
> Listen. Listen to her, child.
> (*HADEJA is silent for a while, until she breaks into a familiar blues tune.*)

CHORUS OF WOMEN:
> Listen, child.

OSHIMI:
> Daughter, hear me.

CHORUS OF WOMEN:
> Hear her. Listen. Child, listen to your mother!

IMO:
> (*Exploding.*) The selling . . .

CHORUS OF WOMEN:
> Must be stopped!

IMO:
> The raping . . .

CHORUS OF WOMEN:
> Must be stopped!

IMO:
> The killing . . .

CHORUS OF WOMEN:
> Must be stopped!

IMO:
> The profiteering . . .

CHORUS OF WOMEN:
> Must be stopped!

IMO:
> The corruption . . .

CHORUS OF WOMEN:
> Must be stopped!

CROSS RIVER:
> Women. This is our fight . . .

OSHIMI:
> Together! This is *our* fight!

IMO:
> Yes, she said it!

HADEJA:
> Said it-said it-said it!

CHORUS OF WOMEN:
> Yes, she said it!

HADEJA:
> So mothers. When do we meet?

CHORUS OF WOMEN:
> Tomorrow!

IMO:
> Yes, tomorrow.

HADEJA:
> We'll march.

CHORUS OF WOMEN:
> March! March! March! (*With* HADEJA *at the center, all the women dance and march toward the GRA/OIL Club until the lights fade into the next stage.*)

MOVEMENT FIVE

(OCEANA, alone. He is smoking in the lounge area when BONNY/PRIEST joins him. Soon after, OMI appears at the gate. OCEANA is obviously uneasy, for he would like to let her in but can't because of his important guest.)

BONNY/PRIEST:
So you know her?

OCEANA:
(Pretending.) Can't see that far now.

BONNY/PRIEST:
You do.

OCEANA:
(Fidgeting.) Ehmm . . . No . . . Ehmmm . . . Used to . . . You know . . . One of those cooks, maybe?

BONNY/PRIEST:
So I see. But know, that's a very loose one. Just be careful.

OCEANA:
(Jokingly.) A loose canon, you mean? *(As their conversation develops, actual voices of the protesters rise slowly in the background. OCEANA listens, sighs, "Oh nothing significant. We'll teach them. They'll have to learn." He waves off the concern and motions to the Priest to resume their chat. OMI, too, is temporarily out of sight as she follows the direction of the rising mob action. OMI reappears again as suddenly as she had disappeared.)*

BONNY/PRIEST:
Whatever. But I'd say steer clear. *(Sighing.)* Women? These times?

OCEANA:
And in these parts?

BONNY/PRIEST:
Native women. Hmm . . . They've changed a lot. Used to be a lot different.

OCEANA:
Really?

BONNY/PRIEST:

Yes. (*Counting.*) Ten whole years. I've been here long enough to know the difference.

OCEANA:

Wao! (*Laughing, crossing over to peep through and to unlock the gate.*) And they haven't offered you a Chieftaincy title yet?

BONNY/PRIEST:

Not quite. But they try . . .

OCEANA:

Quite unlike them. These people. Used to open policies. Always ready for . . .

BONNY/PRIEST:

AIDS?

OCEANA:

That too. They're always willing to give up anything.

BONNY/PRIEST:

But as a good Christian, you must hold up your head above these natives at all times.

OCEANA:

Father, don't I know it? (*Rising mob chants. They listen.*)

BONNY/PRIEST:

Well, just thought I'd remind you. It's getting too hot here.(*He sees the restless OMI reappear at the gate, then sighs.*) These natives! Aaaah!

OCEANA:

I know. (*Pause, puffs at his cigar.*) Except we still have to depend . . . I mean who else would do all these bloody chores?

BONNY/PRIEST:

(*Pours himself a drink.*) Just be careful. *Brethren, know thyself.* That's all.

OCEANA:

I'm completely in control.

BONNY/PRIEST:

(*Rising.*) You should. (*Pause.*) But you know her?

OCEANA:

Hmm . . . yes . . . no (*Pause.*) A domestic help, maybe?

OMI:

(*Hearing this, OMI storms into the scene and brandishes a wristwatch in Oceana's face.*) Oga, you left this inside . . . when you came last night.

OCEANA:

(*Stretching to take it but she pulls back.*) Oh my God. The room!

OMI:

My room.

OCEANA:

You may keep it. For now.

(*OMI drops the watch back in her bag. Silence as OCEANA tries eyeballing and signaling her to leave until the room is clear. But so determined to assert her presence, OMI stands in his face. The Priest is scandalized and looks away. Silence, but for Oceana's whistling. Then OMI again breaks the silence.*)

OMI:

(*To OCEANA.*) Oga, I've come. Anything else you want from me?

OCEANA:

(*Relieved, jumps.*) What do you have to offer?

OMI:

(*Bluffing.*) Beer? Bloody Mary? Gin and lime? Whisky? Brandy? All on the rocks!

OCEANA:

Hmm . . . I'll have the Bloody Mary. (*Fanning himself.*) Too hot in here. (*Turns to the Priest.*) Take something, my friend.

BONNY/PRIEST:

No. Thanks. I'm fine.

OCEANA:

(*Insisting.*) Come on, Father. Have a beer? Some Bloody Mary?

OMI:

(*To the Priest.*) Father, I've got everything you need.

BONNY/PRIEST:

No, thanks.

OCEANA:

Soft drinks? Iced tea? Eggnog? Bournvita?

BONNY/PRIEST:

OK. Ordinary tea will do.

OMI:

Yes, Father.

(*She exits through the door behind OCEANA and soon returns with a tray full of drinks, glasses, a boiling tea kettle, with a cup. With her backside in Oceana's direction, she bends to serve the Priest first.*)

OMI:

(*Pouring the hot tea.*) Father. Like some milk?

BONNY/PRIEST:

Yes. Thanks.

OMI:

(*Pours the milk.*) And sugar?

BONNY/PRIEST:

Sure!

OMI:

I thought so.

(*She quickly dips her hand into her bra, and produces two cubes of sugar.*)

BONNY/PRIEST:

(*Stunned.*) What?

OMI:

(*Smiling.*) Father, you like it sweet. Don't you?

BONNY/PRIEST:

(*Scandalized.*) Yes . . . Oh . . . but . . . Not now. Not any more. Thanks.

OMI:

Father, welcome to Africa!

OCEANA:

(*Laughing.*) These women!

BONNY/PRIEST:

(*The Priest rises.*) I should be going now.

OMI:

(*Pleading.*) Father, stay. If you don't like this one, you can have another . . .

BONNY/PRIEST:

No thanks. Some other time, maybe. (*Turning to OCEANA, who's still so amused.*) I must be going now. And remember, I'll be going back to Europe soon.

OCEANA:

Me too. When are you leaving?

BONNY/PRIEST:

Next week.

OCEANA:

So soon?

BONNY/PRIEST:

Well, about time. It does get lonely out here. And with your deputy in the offshore fields? My friend, take care.

OCEANA:

It does really get lonely. I know.

(*OCEANA escorts his guest to the gate. OMI waves him good-bye and returns to the inner chamber.*)

BONNY/PRIEST:

May God be with you, and guide you.

OCEANA:

Amen. I know He will. Always!

(*BONNY/PRIEST departs. OMI returns to gather the empty glasses. OCEANA trails her loaded chest with his hawkish eyes as he pokes her with a long cigar and nudges her to light it for him. Meanwhile, HADEJA as the Hawker/Seller again appears at the gate with her fruits and chants. Their mother, OSHIMI, soon joins her, together with CROSS RIVER and IKPOBA as an Unemployed Youth, begging and pleading at the gate for employment. OCEANA is so irritated by their noise, he yells at them: "No vacancy. Out! Out of the premises!" But they still plead. Frustrated, OCEANA yells: "Are you deaf? I said no vacancy!" But still they plead their cause. Vexed, OCEANA rises as he threatens: "OK, now, I'll deal with you." At that point, the people begin to hurry out. OMI, who stands frozen and silently watching this development, suddenly drops the tray of glasses, which come crashing down at her feet and Oceana's. For a moment they both stand staring at the broken pieces until their eyes meet and OMI bends down to pick up the pieces. OCEANA, still absorbed in his thoughts, is watching her until he reaches out to her, holds her tenderly, and tries to reassure her with a familiar melody. But OMI is now lost in thought in her own world. She stares at him coldly.*)

OCEANA:

(*Kissing her.*) Troubled, girl? (*OMI, silent and distracted.*) Fear not, says the Lord for I am thy Lord and thy God. And I will be with you till the very end. Just lay your trust in me.

OMI:

(*Rising.*) You know what my mother said?

OCEANA:

Tell me, Babe. What did your Mama say?

OMI:

"Trust no man."

OCEANA:

(*Pulling her down.*) Even me? All men are not the same . . .

OMI:

Not equal. (*YOBE, the Government Official, enters the scene.*)

OCEANA:

And in the eyes of God?

YOBE:

He knows better.

OMI:

Oga, why don't you just leave God out of it?
(*OCEANA is attempting to kiss and fondle again, but OMI is already on her feet, facing the room behind them.*)
I'm hungry.

OCEANA:

For God?

OMI:

(*Playfully, and picking up the tray.*) Are you? You take too much.

YOBE:

Man's lot. Take care, young woman. And be fast. I know your mother . . .

OMI:

Is waiting. Won't be long now.
(*Laughs loud and exits into the room.*)

YOBE:

Good luck. (*Turning to OCEANA.*) Now don't forget tomorrow. Our business . . .

OCEANA:

Hell no! How can I forget? The business is our life.

YOBE:

To control.

OCEANA:

I'm ready.

YOBE:

Always. And that's why I'm here. We have a lot to share, you and I.

OCEANA:

True.

YOBE:

And that is why we must take care of ourselves first. (*He pulls his chair closer to OCEANA.*) You know that man is . . . is funny?

OCEANA:

Which man?

YOBE:

The Chief, you know.

OCEANA:

(*Scribbling at a signpost.*) Hmmm . . . Oh yes! Oh, yes!

YOBE:

You trust him?

OCEANA:

Hmm . . . ?

YOBE:

You do.

OCEANA:

(*Pretending.*) What?

YOBE:

I say do you trust the Chief?

OCEANA:

(*Smiling.*) Oh, that? (*Hesitates.*) Yeah, as much as the weather.

YOBE:

Oh, come on, you seem to like him a lot. Do a lot of business with him.

OCEANA:

Do I have a choice? He's their Traditional Thief . . . Pardon, Chief. (*Pause.*) And by the way, where's that gypsy?

YOBE:

The girl?

OCEANA:

The boy. The guard. (*He presses the button by his side. No response. Repeats. No response.*) Monkeying around, probably.

YOBE:

Or sleeping.

OCEANA:

You know them. Always sleeping on the job. (*Peeps into the security post.*)

YOBE:

Not in his place?

OCEANA:

He's gone. (*Sighs.*) These black . . . Oh Boy! Always the same response. (*Mimicking.*) "Sir he's not on seat—not on seat." When will they ever be on heat?

YOBE:

Seat! (*Chuckles.*)

OCEANA:
> Whatever!

YOBE:
> Never. (*Pause.*) And that girl too. I know how you feel. Ehm . . . ehm . . .
> I don't want to get into your business. But be careful. None of these peo-
> ple can be trusted.

OCEANA:
> (*Loud laughter.*) You telling me? Of course I know. Can't you see I'm
> always checking?
> (*Steals glances at YOBE, who is digging the ground to mount the post.*)

YOBE:
> I don't blame you. It's too risky.

OCEANA:
> Yes. Here. Too risky to trust.

YOBE:
> But it's all part of it. (*Silence.*) But trust me, I have a special offer. Let's
> make a deal.
> (*Stunned, OCEANA stares at him. Silence.*)
> You know the new offshore line? (*Silence.*)

OCEANA:
> (*Suspicious.*) Hmm . . . Yes.

YOBE:
> We can make a fortune . . . You and I . . .

OCEANA:
> What?

YOBE:
> (*Smiling.*) Pump a million barrels or more a day. No records. Ships wait-
> ing at sea. Sale sealed. Paid in dollars or pound sterling overseas into
> your account and mine. No hassles. Just that we'll have to displace more
> villagers.

OCEANA:
> (*Animated.*) Easily!

YOBE:
> Yes.

OCEANA:
> Order them to move out . . . to . . . to . . . But where to?

YOBE:
> I know. The camp is bursting full. And there's been no running water
> for one year. No light and other amenities either.

OCEANA:
Diseased. A cesspool of epidemics.

YOBE:
Cholera gains . . .

OCEANA:
Well, we can't help it. They'll have to figure it out by themselves.

YOBE:
One way or the other.

OCEANA:
Right! (*Pause.*) But honestly, your idea sounds good to me.

YOBE:
Really?

OCEANA:
Great.

YOBE:
(*Exuberantly.*) Think. You and I work for governments . . . for companies. We're not getting younger, you know? Time passes. Daily we're working our butts off. At home we have a saying that the horn-blower also has the need to blow his nose. Yes! (*OCEANA smiles.*) Government company pays itself. We, too, must learn to pay ourselves. First. (*Watching to let the idea sink in.*)

OCEANA:
(*Hesitating.*) Hmm . . . makes sense . . . And why not? Great . . . Sounds like a good idea. (*Pause.*) One thing, though. I don't trust . . . I mean . . . feel safe with anyone . . . I mean . . . Can't you see the look of hate in these people's eyes? Even the domestic servants who work for you!

YOBE:
I know what you mean. In our position we can't ever be too careful.

OCEANA:
I'm glad you understand. The tone is changing here. It used to be much more comfortable. But these days. These youths? And even the women?

YOBE:
Don't worry. We'll take care of them.

OCEANA:
How? What do you propose?

YOBE:
(*Pensive.*) Hmm . . . Government is not blind or asleep, you know. We have secret agents. Constant armed surveillance. We use the police too to check.

OCEANA:

So you know the troublemakers?

YOBE:

Precisely! No government should be taken for granted. We're keeping our records. The General orders that no stone be left unturned.

OCEANA:

What precisely? What concrete plans?

YOBE:

Oh well, we have our secret agents right there with them in the market-place.

OCEANA:

Great!

YOBE:

We'll silence anybody who dares speak against, challenge, or sabotage our government. We've dispatched our boys into all nooks and corners of the land. Even in the marketplace.

OCEANA:

Ah, those rowdy traders!

(*PIPELINE, the Chief, approaches now, but they are not aware.*)

YOBE:

Well, the bottom line is . . . I mean with all the sacrifices we're making, it's only fair that we pay ourselves first.

OCEANA:

(*Chuckling.*) Earn as you work.

YOBE:

Yeah! It's a deal.

OCEANA:

Sounds reasonable to me.

YOBE:

(*Playfully.*) Earn as you work.

OCEANA:

Right! The best I've learned so far! (*Warm handshakes.*)

YOBE:

Our share. It's a deal!

(*Suddenly PIPELINE, the Chief, enters. They're startled.*)

PIPELINE:

(*Laughing.*) And my share too!

OCEANA:

(*Stammering.*): Wha . . . wha . . . You . . . Your share?

YOBE:

What share?

PIPELINE:

I heard something about shares. (*OMI peeps from her corner, but they don't see her.*) I too want mine. Yes. My share!

OCEANA:

Oh no. Not now . . . Not now, my friend. Ehm . . . (*Coughs.*) You mis . . . misread . . . mis . . . heard

PIPELINE:

Oh no.

YOBE:

Well, misspoke. (*Coughs.*) Ehm . . . Chief! (*Praising.*) Our great Chief! Lord of the land!

OCEANA:

(*Recovering.*) The land lord!

PIPELINE:

That's me! Yes my share. Whoever works has to get a share.

YOBE:

True, true. But you're wrong. You didn't hear right.

PIPELINE:

What? No shares?

YOBE:

Nothing. Nothing to share. At least not now.

OCEANA:

(*Recovering.*) Except the responsibilities.

PIPELINE:

Those too. But my ears heard right. You know the blind man says he's heard people talking about sharing. So unless the whole thing is divided again he's not going to accept it.
(*They laugh.*)

YOBE:

(*Teasing.*) Oh, Chief. Funny man. Always asking for *your* share. Makes one think of you as a tax collector.

OCEANA:

Are you, Chief?
(*They all laugh. YOBE rises.*)

YOBE:

I must be going now. Time for the Cabinet Meeting.

PIPELINE:

Make sure you tell them about us. Represent our interest.

YOBE:
> Always. Always.

OCEANA:
> (*A handshake with* YOBE.) *Our* interest. Remember?

YOBE:
> My word!
> (*Exit* YOBE. OCEANA *walks back to the lounge. The Chief follows. They sit.*)

PIPELINE:
> (*Coughs.*) These Government Officials! Never trust them.

OCEANA:
> True? I've heard that a billion times.

PIPELINE:
> (*Whispering.*) I tell you, be careful.

OCEANA:
> But why precisely?

PIPELINE:
> They're greedy. Oh so greedy! (*Coughs, adjusts his seat.*) Government workers working for themselves. Ha! Ha! Ha!

OCEANA:
> (*Laughing.*) You all . . . I know. Ha!

PIPELINE:
> That's why you must listen to me. (*Pause.*) You see that new place by my village where you just struck a new oil well? (OCEANA *is silently studying him.*) Well, the people there too are my own people.

OCEANA:
> Meaning?

PIPELINE:
> Compensation.

OCEANA:
> Oh yes! We'll compensate the people as usual.

PIPELINE:
> Yes. Pay. Through *me.*

OCEANA:
> How much?

PIPELINE:
> You know, the usual thing.

OCEANA:
> But it's a very small well.

PIPELINE:

(*Laughing.*) Yes, as they say, "the swallow's smile can only be as big as his mouth." Not so?

OCEANA:

Hmmm . . . You people and your proverbs! Well, I guess . . . I do.

PIPELINE:

So make the payments in *my* name. I'm their leader, after all.

OCEANA:

But Chief. You need to understand the way government works.

PIPELINE:

Oh, don't tell me that. I know. Remember I too was in government? Yes, a civil servant. I slaved . . . My friend, a government *slave*. That is what a civil servant means.

OCEANA:

I hear you. But the rule with the government is that all compensations should go to the community to ensure that everyone is paid. You know everyone in that village must be displaced to the camp . . . moved to the camp. Nothing there yet.

PIPELINE:

Oh, yes. They will get . . . I mean, through me. I'm their Chief, their leader. No one goes to the community . . . land . . . except through me. And no one comes to it or to you, except through me.

OCEANA:

(*Chuckling.*) The millennium messiah!

PIPELINE:

Sure! I am the way. The truth . . .

OCEANA:

But not the life?

PIPELINE:

Oh, yes. I am. Everything!

OCEANA:

Yeah, the deity. Ha! No one goes to heaven alive. (*They laugh.*) And so you got everyone coming and going. (*More laughter.*)

PIPELINE:

That's it!

OCEANA:

And you must write your own ticket.

PIPELINE:

Yes. Here. Right here!
(*He pushes a sheet of paper. OCEANA studies it, alarmed.*)

OCEANA:
Isn't this too much?

PIPELINE:
The cost of everything's going up, you know. Inflation.

OCEANA:
That I understand. But here the rate of inflation's higher than that of production.
(*PIPELINE is silent, then resolves.*)

PIPELINE:
OK. Pay a million then. Half for the community. The other half to me personally (*OCEANA is stunned, silent.*) Yes, fair enough. That will do, for the incidental costs. You never know. As we say, the farmer who goes to the farm must be armed with enough drinking water. You cannot cry without eyes. Can you?

OCEANA:
I guess not. Hmm . . . Interesting . . . OK, you got a deal.

PIPELINE:
And one more deal to keep you smiling all the way to the bank.

OCEANA:
Yes. Be quick.

PIPELINE:
I know. "*Deal's*" your other name.

OCEANA:
No apologies. Isn't that what we're here for?

PIPELINE:
OK. (*Coughs, clears his throat, and draws near.*) In addition to my brother's daughter, Imo . . .

OCEANA:
Who?

PIPELINE:
Our daughter that I gave to your European friend. (*Silence.*) Or you've forgotten?

OCEANA:
Which? No. My American brother? Sure I remember! So what about her?

PIPELINE:
Nothing. Just to say she's fine . . . Yes . . . fine . . . and pleased . . .

OCEANA:
Had to be. That guy . . .

PIPELINE:
A multibillionaire, I hear.

OCEANA:
Great guy. He can buy the entire Third World. (*Drinks.*) That girl is lucky.

PIPELINE:
Very lucky. (*Pause, scratches his head.*) Hmm . . . and that is why I must give you another. One good turn deserves another. Isn't that what they say?

OCEANA:
Oh, yes. (*Thinking.*) That other girl . . . I mean your daughter. How's she anyway? Do you hear from her?

PIPELINE:
Regularly. Tells me it's winter . . . deadly cold over there now.

OCEANA:
That is true.

PIPELINE:
She complains.

OCEANA:
Really?

PIPELINE:
Says she wants to come back. You know women. Like to . . . ehm . . . always complaining. What men have to bear! Ha!

OCEANA:
Imo. "Fun girl she was," so my brother wrote. I'm surprised.

PIPELINE:
That is why I'm offering this other one . . .

OCEANA:
What? Who?

PIPELINE:
A sweet daughter of the land. Take. Take her to Europe . . . I mean to America for your next recess. I know how important it is for a hard-working man to relax. Ha! What are friends for, after all? You'll be blessed with this one.

OCEANA:
Women . . .

PIPELINE:
Evil.

OCEANA:
Partners.

PIPELINE:
Necessary evil.

OCEANA:
That's why you have so many?

PIPELINE:
What can we do? Man must wack! (*Chuckles.*) You'll be blessed with this one.

OCEANA:
But Chief. You can see my hands are full. My wife's out there, you know. And now . . .

PIPELINE:
Hadeja!

OCEANA:
Omi.

PIPELINE:
No. Hadeja. Her sister.

OCEANA:
The hawker?

PIPELINE:
Got it!

OCEANA:
Her?

PIPELINE:
Young. Juicy. Makes a man . . . (*Coughs.*) Jump . . .

OCEANA:
I'm tired, man.

PIPELINE:
Goes with the territory. Women . . . (*Pause.*) Take her. Take her.

OCEANA:
Hmm . . . Let me think.

PIPELINE:
Feel free to pass her on to any of your friends over there. All I ask in return is that you pass on your Landcruiser to me.

OCEANA:
(*Stunned.*) What? My Landcruiser?

PIPELINE:

Yes. A very modest price for such a delicious offering . . . I mean gift . . . Most fertile land, my friend. Count your blessings.

OCEANA:

As you like it. But what do you need this one for? You still have the other Pathfinder you took for the other one . . . that Imo girl.

PIPELINE:

That was one deal. This is another. Not so?

OCEANA:

I guess. (*Pause.*) So when is she coming?

PIPELINE:

Name your day.

OCEANA:

Anytime soon?

PIPELINE:

At your pleasure!

OCEANA:

If you insist.

PIPELINE:

I do. The *Landlord,* remember?

OCEANA:

Sure always.

(*They shake hands. Exit* PIPELINE. *He ruminates. Alone. Shortly after his departure,* OMI, *draped with the white sheet from the lounge table, crawls out of hiding and hastens to the Market-Square. Then lights pick up* PIPELINE, *the Chief, who's now alone on his way home from the GRA/Oil Club. He appears to be troubled.*)

PIPELINE:

(*Alone.*) Imo? Yes. That deaf daughter. "Eneke nti mkpo." Deaf! Deaf like that Eneke bird. Since she left for the white man's land, I haven't heard from that girl. Not even a word to say, "Here, uncle. Take this dollar or pound sterling to buy yourself some tobacco, snuff, soap, or oil to grease your chapped . . ." Oh, these children! Except just for a few who do remember that you labored for them. A lot of children are so ungrateful. So self-centered. Always taking and taking and expecting parents to do even more and more. (*Deep sigh.*) What losses parents suffer? You labor, hope to gain out of your own investment. But all you get back is nothing. Nothing! (*Fuming, his pace quickens now.*) I'm going to write to that senseless girl. Tell her what her mates abroad are doing at home, especially in the cities. Mansions here. Mansions there. Expensive estates springing up like mushrooms everywhere. Been to the banks lately? A new spectacle. No room to breathe. The once wretched mothers and fathers now choke the air as they'd line up to collect the thousands and thousands of foreign money sent to them by their children abroad. But not my own. No, not mine. Stupid girl! She's forgotten me. Drinking tea, milk, and all the juices from those White men. Ha! (*Spits.*) Shame! Shame on you, Imo! You who go to the White man's land to forget your very own. This is the day. I must . . . must write and tell her my mind. Do something now or never. Ungrateful child. After all I've done for her since they killed her father? And then her mother? That Jesse oil hell fire? The struggle for oil? Take . . . taken . . . so many. Aaaah . . . (*Pause.*) And I just wanted to help. Help her from the hell. . . . Now what has she given to pay me back? Nothing. Nothing but disgrace . . . pain . . . Ah! That girl will pay back . . . And if not, she'll cease to be mine . . . Not even in death for I will disown her. Thank God she's only a girl. Could you imagine her as a son to whom I'd have to bestow my own line . . . legacy? No way! (*Pause, smiles.*) This other daughter . . . Hadeja, I mean, is the answer to line my empty pockets. Yes. I need another car. Yes! I'm selling . . . God I'm "sending" her with him . . . the White man. That crafty man who has so much but still counts every penny he gives or pays for anything. God! They're so stingy, these foreigners! Well, I too will get . . . my share . . . *My* share! And that's it. All I want. To make it up . . . (*His face suddenly lights up.*) Aaah, Hadeja! Hadeja, honey— sweet as freshly brewed wine in the morning dew.(*Smacking his lips.*) Nice. Juicy like the succulent fruits she sells. Oh, such a great diet! And as I grabbed her fruits? Split open? And bit into that succulent pulp? Ha! She struggled, struggled, and cried out loud to be saved. Saved? From what, baptism? Indeed, that's all it was. A baptism. For I could tell from the thick and narrow walls inside that the fruit was still green. Until I bit into it. Chaam! Ha!

(*He quickens his pace towards his home as OMI crosses to the other side of the Market-Square.*)

OMI:

(*Frantic.*) I'm going to tell . . . Mother . . . Imo . . . Ikpoba? Ah! I'll take him now to that place. Teach them a lesson. Let the war begin! Now! Now's the time to do it. And my sister, Hadeja? My God, where's she? Where? Just hope she's not returning to sell in that place. No! (*Running.*) Sister, I'm with you. Now! All the way. You'll never be alone again. Never! I'll be with you till the very end. Oh, God, I'm coming! I'm going. Now!

(*Running. The lights lead her home to the next stage.*)

MOVEMENT SIX

(OMI returns to the GRA/Oil Club, where OCEANA and YOBE, the Government Official, are meeting. They are signing some documents, but as soon as they see her coming, they quickly dash into the room with the files. OMI waits outside, humming a somber tune until the men return and let her in. Just then, two young men [one of them is IKPOBA wearing a mask] try to open the iron gate. But they can't. They bow and plead several times, hoping that OCEANA and YOBE will let them in, but they simply give them a nasty glare until the disgusted OCEANA rises and blows his whistle. Immediately his guard BONNY/GUARD X storms the scene from behind, salutes his master, and awaits his orders.)

OCEANA:
Arrest those robbers!

BONNY/GUARD X:
Yes saar!

OCEANA:
Teach them a hard lesson.

BONNY/GUARD X:
Yes saar!

(BONNY/GUARD X makes a quick dash for the youths. The one arrested is IKPOBA, while the other flees with a scream: "See you tomorrow!" The arrested youth pleads frantically for freedom and mercy. "I no do anytin. I no be tief. I no fuck him wife. Na only job I want. Na only food. Just food I dey find. I beg. I beg, broda, help me. Help me beg am. Beg Oyiboman for me. Na beg I dey beg!" His pleading and protestations continue as the youth is dragged through the door behind, followed with a loud noise. YOBE departs hurriedly. OCEANA leans back again to light a cigar. He reaches out for the radio, tunes into a slow jam music station as he continues to smoke and pace up and down in his deep thought.)

OCEANA:
(To OMI.) Come now, sugar! *(OMI is silent but agitated.)*

OCEANA:

(*Puffing away smoke.*) Do come now. What was he saying?

OMI:

You mean *crying*?

OCEANA:

Same to me . . . Their crying and talking. They blame me for . . .

OMI:

Nothing. Just nothing. You are beyond blame. It's just us. We are the problem.

OCEANA:

(*Studying her.*) True. Baby, you're so honest, so different from everyone else. (*Pause. Smokes.*) Only sometimes I can't . . . don't understand . . . I mean especially with that young man. After all, they're your people.

OMI:

I know. (*Reassuring smiles.*) No problem. It's not me you should fear.

OCEANA:

But whom?

OMI:

Nobody. After all, are you no longer in control?

OCEANA:

Certainly.

OMI:

So why fear . . . ?

OCEANA:

(*Thinking.*) Control? (*Pause.*) But these people . . .

OMI:

I know.

OCEANA:

Don't trust . . . I mean soon, you too might be telling me he's your brother. And that one is your uncle. (*Chuckling.*) You black women and your imaginary brothers and uncles! Ha!

(*They're interrupted by the wailing of the youth inside the cell. Outside, sounds of protests are also rising and drawing nearer. OMI fights her anxiety and rage. OCEANA is trying to pull her to his bosom, but she resists.*)

OMI:

Oga, please release me. Let me go.

(*She hums a tune: "Please Release Me."*)

OCEANA:

I have you. Where do you think you're going?

OMI:

Home.

OCEANA:

Where? (*Loud laughter.*)

OMI:

My place.

OCEANA:

Where's that? (*Laughs.*) Don't be ridiculous. You belong here . . . in my arms.

OMI:

To rule?

OCEANA:

Damn the rules! All I want is my own . . .

OMI:

(*Cursing in her language.*) *Death*! No. Quick, o'jare! Let me go? Stop wasting my bloody time.

OCEANA:

What? (*Silence.*) What did you say?

OMI:

Nothing . . . Yet. (*Explodes into laughter.*)

OCEANA:

You silly girl. Why be in such a rush?

OMI:

(*Reading her watch.*) It's time. Time. I'm done.

OCEANA:

(*Angry.*) With me?

OMI:

Oh, come on. Don't take it personally. Time respects no king or master. I have to go. My people . . .

OCEANA:

Your people?

OMI:

(*Laughing.*) Who else? It's been so long. My mother is waiting. I have to go . . .

OCEANA:

Join them?

OMI:

>   (*Laughs, plays with his chin.*) To get paid!

OCEANA:

>   Not now. You have to wait.

OMI:

>   Till when? How long?

OCEANA:

>   But tell me, why are you in such a hurry now?

OMI:

>   (*More agitated.*) But I've been here, waiting all this time. I'm tired. See you. (*Picks up her shoes.*)

OCEANA:

>   Why are you acting up? You crazy?

OMI:

>   (*Snapping.*) To you. Just pay me.

OCEANA:

>   Money. That's all?

OMI:

>   Yes! A worker expects to be paid. Is that too much to ask *the* director?

OCEANA:

>   Maybe not. But . . . (*Checks himself.*) You're not . . . not just a worker. And after all these special moments? Don't you think you mean more . . . I mean, more than a worker? Babe, you need to think better of yourself.

OMI:

>   Does that put money into my pocket? Feed me? Pay the bills?

OCEANA:

>   Hey, wait a minute. This talk about money-money-money! Pay-pay-pay! Is that all there is to it? All that you people think about?

OMI:

>   That's all. What else do hungry people think about?

OCEANA:

>   But Babe, you're not like them. You're different. (*Silence.*) So different. Why this sudden change?

OMI:

>   Your teaching. Ha! Ha! Ha!

OCEANA:

>   But haven't I been treating . . . taking care of you?

OMI:

> That you have. But don't you think I can do it better for myself? Instead of having to depend . . . (*Pause.*) Anyway, I'm on my way now. Got to move on!
> (*She picks up her bag.*)

OCEANA:

> Babe, I don't understand you anymore. What are you trying to say?

OMI:

> Precisely what I just said. I'm ready. On my way now.

OCEANA:

> You may. It's your choice. I can't help . . . give you anything now.

OMI:

> So when?

OCEANA:

> Not until you behave . . . know yourself.

OMI:

> I see. (*Tersely.*) Oceana, I need my money and I need to go. Now!
> (*Silence as they stand staring at each other.*)

OCEANA:

> Do as you please.

OMI:

> (*Smiling, walking away.*) OK, I'll be back.

OCEANA:

> (*Pulling her back.*) Silly girl! One of your mood swings again? You know just how I feel about . . . Oh, well, tell me you're not leaving.

OMI:

> (*Smiling.*) I said it already. I *will* be back.

OCEANA:

> I will be waiting here, Babe. And tell me you won't be long.

OMI:

> (*Hesitates, smiles.*) OK. I won't.
> (*Spotlights following her. She steadily walks away without looking back. OCEANA escorts her with his lustful eyes. Once she's gone, he slumps into the lounge chair, lights a cigarette, and starts puffing away smoke. Alone.*)

OCEANA:

> (*Sighs.*) She's been acting up lately. Hmm . . . Who knows? Who knows what's eating her up? So young? I thought I'd find peace with this one. They're usually better young, juicy, easier to manage. At least before

they grow into that premenopausal phase. Ha! The moon phase I call it! I know it, I can see it coming. Yes, I saw it in my first wife, Judy. Then Katie. And now this one? But she's too young . . . Oh, well, women . . . never too young to give a man heartaches. I've had it with them. Whatever you do as a man, you can never please them. Strange. Strange. Women! And this breed here? Even stranger.(*The gate cracks open. In a swift movement, OMI crosses behind. Startled, not exactly sure of what he saw, OCEANA walks to the iron gate to check and reinforce the lock. Meanwhile, OMI goes behind to release her lover, IKPOBA. But for the birds chirping and his dog barking, everything appears calm as he returns, pours himself a drink, and continues musing.*) Actually reminds me of my wife at home. Who knows what she's doing now? Been acting up even more lately. Must be having her usual shopping spree. Katie . . . "Born to Shop." That should have been her name. (*Parodying her.*) "Oh, darling! Just this one more diamond. I want it. Now. Just this." (*Guffaws.*) Ha! What can you do but be a man . . . and yield? To her, yes. But not this one. (*Chuckles.*) Cute . . . My Cutie! I just love her . . . Much like the child I should have . . . but never had. (*Pause.*) I wish . . . Well, too late now. Maybe it's the reason I want her so . . . So bad. Does she . . . Does she really know that I care? Well, what does it matter? She's just another country girl. We've been warned. Told not to give these natives, especially their girls, the impression that we have money and yield to their demands. They'll get spoiled. Start expecting too much. And when you stop? Ha! Sour grapes! No. Can't risk that. A woman's wrath? Beware, man. Beware! If you come out of it alive. You'll never be the same. Scalded. For life. Been there, done that! So this one too expects me to yield to blackmail? No way. I won't . . . Let a woman take advantage of me? No! No more! (*Pause.*) But I've got to keep on playing. (*Looks at his watch.*) My God, how time flies! Soon I'll be gone. Write her, Katie? My wife . . . My life . . . (*Another look at his watch.*)

(*Sits and starts writing when suddenly, OMI storms back into the scene to confront OCEANA. He jumps, screams, "My Gaaad!"*)

OMI:

(*In his face.*) Here! My time. Get ready!

OCEANA:

I'll be damned! How did you get in here?

OMI:

Don't ask. Just pay. Pay me.

OCEANA:

What's come over you? You crazy?

OMI:

Right. Pay me.

OCEANA:

I see. (*Silence as* OCEANA *stands gazing at her, until he explodes.*) You too? Ungrateful b . . . ! Harassing me after all I've given . . . done for you?

OMI:

You've done nothing. Given nothing.

OCEANA:

(*Mock laughter.*) Really?

OMI:

Yes!

OCEANA:

Ok. My gold watch? Give it back.

OMI:

(*Flinging it.*) That's it. Take. As if that's important. Ha! Ha! Ha! You think I care? I don't!

OCEANA:

(*Stunned.*) I can't believe this. Omi? You? You too? well, I'll be damned! (*Sighs.*) I thought you were . . . were not like these people. (*Silence.*) But . . . but tell me . . . What . . . what . . . What is it you want?

OMI:

What you owe.

OCEANA:

(*Exploding.*) Dammit! I owe you nothing. Nothing!

OMI:

Really? You'll soon find out.

OCEANA:

(*Furious.*) Out! (*OMI is smiling but defiant.*) You get on my nerves! You're just like them. Another piece of trash. Get out of here. Now!

OMI:

Don't you touch me!

OCEANA:

What? Who are you?

OMI:

(*Calmly.*) You'll soon find out.

OCEANA:

What nonsense! (*He steps forward to push her.*)

OMI:

Try! Just dare to touch me. And you'll be sorry for it . . . Everything!

OCEANA:

(*Shocked.*) So this is it? (*Pause.*) But I don't blame you. It's me . . . my mistake. I trusted . . . invested in . . . in . . . nothing. (*Reflecting.*) And all I got is suckers. Suckers!

OMI:

(*Mock laughter.*) Like you, sir. You taught us well.

OCEANA:

Godammit! I paid for it . . . for everything! Nonsense! You people suck. Nothing but suckers. Never to render any service with . . . without inflating . . . satisfaction.

OMI:

Is it by force?

OCEANA:

What the hell am I doing with this fuc . . . illiterate . . . ?

OMI:

(*Smiling.*) I've seen your betters.

OCEANA:

And you think I haven't? Ha! This nation of crooks and bastards!

OMI:

(*In his face.*) You people. All you want is to get something out of nothing. Not so?

OCEANA:

What? Look who's talking. The sucker herself! I paid my dues . . . fully.

OMI:

To whom? No, you haven't. You owe your life to us . . . this very land.

OCEANA:

You land of liars! Stinking debtor-nation. Aren't you ashamed? All potentials and morality sold. Auctioned to the highest bidder. Out of my sight! Bitch!

OMI:

(*Strutting.*) Call me what you like. But beware.

OCEANA:

Me?

OMI:

(*Emphatically.*) Yes, you *beware.* You can't take me or anyone here for a ride anymore. No. No more jolly rides, you white master!

OCEANA:

That's easy. You'll see!

OMI:

Dare!

(*She sits on the lounge chair and dares him to push her out. Behind them, IKPOBA escapes with Oceana's gun, BONNY/GUARD X following behind him.*)

OCEANA:

You get on my nerves. Get out! Out of my sight! You're trespassing on my property!

OMI:

Trespassing? On *my* land! Ha! Albino. You are joking!

(*OCEANA is so enraged, he starts looking for his gun.*)

OCEANA:

Just wait. We'll know who rules . . . (*Tries to push her out.*)

OMI:

Don't you dare touch me!

OCEANA:

(*Advancing threateningly.*) I will. (*Smokes.*) But you're only a woman. I'll have to restrain myself . . . Restraint, a scarce commodity in this savage land. Yes!

OMI:

(*Defiantly.*) Your concern? Just try me! Ha! Ha! Ha!

OCEANA:

What for? You worthless . . .

OMI:

(*Hysterical laughter.*) Ha! Ha! Ha! We'll see.

OCEANA:

Are you threatening me? Remember who you are talking to? I'm the Director of Sh . . .

OMI:

(*Saluting.*) Precisely. The *Director of Hell!*

OCEANA:

You'll be sorry for this. All of you.

OMI:

Sorry for what?

OCEANA:

(*Dials the phone.*) I'm calling Headquarters for security reinforcement. Get ready.

OMI:

And who says we're not?

OCEANA:

OK. We'll see who wins this war.

OMI:

(*Mock laughter.*) We'll see! We are the bastards, remember? My friend, pay. Pay up your debts.

OCEANA:

Who's your friend?

OMI:

OK, my enemy then. Better still. Pay up.

OCEANA:

I don't owe you a thing, you worthless pros . . .

OMI:

I'm worthless to you now because I want my rights?

OCEANA:

Your . . . ? Nonsense! I'm giving nothing. If you don't like my decision, then too bad. Or better still, go to court. I'm ready.

OMI:

Really? Then get ready.

(*She explodes into laughter, stops suddenly, and confronts him.*)

Like you too, master, I fix my price for my buyers. Don't you fix the price for the goods you sell to us? Do we dictate the price for you to sell? So why should it be different for us? You come to our own land. You take and take and also dictate the price? And still we have no rights to say "no"? Haba, Monsieur le Directeur! Where is your avowed justice? Where is your fairness? A deal is a deal.

OCEANA:

A deal? With whom?

OMI:

With you, man!

OCEANA:

Ridiculous.

OMI:

To you, I fix my price: $5? $10? And all night long, everything adds up. (*Vulgarly displaying her body. OCEANA is now completely disgusted and moves away as he smokes and observes her with scorn.*) You touch? $10. Suck? A double blow. And then the big one? Ah, Mr. Director? You think you can just continue to pour and discharge all that for nothing? And then AIDS? Add that too. Ah, Oga, Director! What if? What if? And then

the other risk? Unwanted baby. My dear, will . . . Will you raise the baby? *Our* baby? No, you won't. All you want is just to kick us around and out . . . to clean up your mess . . . To drain . . . To drill . . . No, man. Not any more! You pour it? You pay for it! You pump it? You pay for it. You mess it up? *You* clean it up!
(*Silence as the incredulous* OCEANA *smokes and observes from a corner while she takes center stage.*)
Or what do you think I am? A piece of stone?

OCEANA:

(*Rises, grabs the phone.*) Shit! Can't take it anymore.

OMI:

You wanted it. Brought me here. Paid me pennies all day and you want to kiss? Pay up, man. All day long you took my bra. My panties, you put under your pillow and you've been sniffing and sniffing and touching and sucking . . . And then you poured all that into . . . God! Don't you know it costs money? You think I'm worth nothing? Well, I tell you now, Oyibo, you've taken and taken. It's about time. Now. Pay up. We don't run charities here. Isn't that what you say? Well, hear. I'm no Charity. My name is Omi. Nothing goes for nothing. That's what you taught us. You know what that means? I know you don't. Better go find out because I'm not just a mere local chicken that you pluck out her plumes and throw into your bowl of soup to eat just like that. Oh, no. You *can't* continue to eat me for nothing, you Director of Hell! You've sucked and drained enough. Now pay up, man!

OCEANA:

You're just a slut. That's all. I picked you up. Remember?

OMI:

And is that why you must devalue . . . I mean make me lose my entire worth and self-respect? Ah, man. Even a prostitute has her dignity and humanity.

OCEANA:

Look who's talking! Did you ever have any?

OMI:

(*Takes out a scroll of paper from her bag.*) Look. I have my degrees.

OCEANA:

(*Startled, jumps.*) A what?

OMI:

I said *degrees*!

OCEANA:

What? You kidding! Can't . . . can't be right.
(*He sits back, contemplating this new development.*)

OMI:

Well, I am. I didn't speak with water in my mouth, did I? (*Lifting the papers like some sacred testament.*) Yes, degrees. Not one, but two. Worked my butt off to earn them both. BSC, MSC. (*Deep sigh.*) Like you too, I have them. Earned them. And many others like me in this land . . . with a load of degrees! But see? Where are we now? Where? You have the upper hand because your country lifts you up. And mine abandons, forsakes, betrays me . . . all of us . . . with you in control . . .

OCEANA:

So . . . so . . . ?

OMI:

God decrees fairness! Look, White man. If not for this condition we're in? No jobs . . . no amenities . . . no rights . . . (*Sighs.*) Just this permanent condition of joblessness. Ah! You think I'll be here hawking my precious body to earn a living? And you, squeezing and taking undue advantage of me . . . of us . . . and everything? Just who do you think you are?

OCEANA:

(*Smiling, smoking.*) The director. (*Crosses his legs.*) The one and only authority in charge here. Hey, won't you thank me for my sacrifices? Risking my precious life to make . . . manage your resources? This bloody country without a leader? Don't you ever blame me. I take what I can get. After all, your so-called leaders gave me the power.

OMI:

No. Only the contracts!

OCEANA:

(*Laughing.*) What's the difference between contracts and power? (*OMI stares at him spitefully.*) Woman, tell me. What is? Ha! Ha! Ha! Better know it. Interests rule the world.

OMI:

Self-interest . . .

OCEANA:

Right! Don't you think I too have a right to seek mine? Protect my own interests?

OMI:

At whose expense? Mine? Our land? The impoverished women and youths?

OCEANA:
Does it matter? And who cares?

OMI:
Oh, hear him! (*Parodying.*) Ha! "Does it matter?" No it *doesn't*! So let's exchange positions; you take mine. I take yours. Exchange is no robbery. Isn't that what they say?

OCEANA:
(*Laughing.*) Woman, I can see that you are suffering from an acute strain of Idealism. An acute deficiency of Realism, rather. And I sympathize with you. But be advised. In today's world, one thing sells fast: Capitalism, forged on individual, private interest, seasoned by national ... No, my dear. Idealism ... communal ... well, communism ... a ready formula for loss, perpetual want, denials, and bankruptcy. It just can't, and won't, sell. A very high-risk venture capital that just won't sell in our wired world today.

OMI:
Hence you bind us, hands and feet?

OCEANA:
No. Tell you what. Try the emerging global market. To succeed? Profit. Profit. Profit. The new creed of success. That's the new Reality. Trust me. It sells. And sells at high costs in today's stock market. Young woman, look at it this way. You can't take your hopes and Idealism to the bank. Can you? But Reality. The real stock ... ?

OMI:
Hello! You just proved my point. Reality is me. Now. So pay me. I'm ready to go to the bank!

OCEANA:
(*Smiling.*) But woman. Don't you know I am the bank you have to go to? I am the director, remember?

OMI:
Whose? Not mine.
(*OCEANA finally loses his temper and yells "Out!" He pushes her. OMI falls, rises and confronts him as he struggles to overcome her.*)

OCEANA:
Guard! Guard! Come and get this sucker out of here. (*No response. The struggle continues.*) That fool. Where is he now?

OMI:
Are you asking me?

OCEANA:
He's your bloody countryman. Is he not? You planned this. A setup.

(*OCEANA tries to reach the closet to pull out his gun, but OMI shouts something to BONNY/GUARD X in their local language. There is no answer; both BONNY/GUARD X and her lover, IKPOBA, have gone to join the mob.*)

OCEANA:
Shut up!

OMI:
No, you can't. I'm through. Not in my land! Our land! Oyibo. You are a visitor. A guest must not be allowed to sit on top of the owners of the land, suffocate them, and then take away the seat with him as he goes . . .

OCEANA:
(*Frustrated.*) Guard! Guard! (*Silence.*) That guard? He's fired! Fired! That idiot? Fired! He'll never work for me any more. Gooooolie! These people. Can't trust them. (*Grabs her.*)

OMI:
And you? Can we trust you? Hey! Makes us equal. You taught us well. (*With both of them locked in each other's arms, the militant chants grow urgent, nearer. OCEANA listens, terror-stricken. His arms fall, limp. OMI is now free.*)

OCEANA:
(*Alarmed.*) You . . . you . . . gang . . . set up . . . Is it?

OMI:
My time!

(*She bursts into laughter as her lover, IKPOBA, and BONNY/GUARD X, storm the gate with the mob in a nonviolent protest. They're clamoring, banging at the locked gate. OCEANA stands stupefied, frozen. OMI hurries to join the mob as they cheer, jeer, and mock OCEANA, with some women dressed like him in tie and shirt. He recovers, briefly, then grabs the phone to call YOBE. Blackout.*)

MOVEMENT SEVEN

(Same location at the GRA/Oil Club. OCEANA, PIPELINE, the Chief, and YOBE, the Government Official, are in conference. The people's drumbeats keep throbbing in the background. OCEANA is worried and exasperated.)

YOBE:

This is getting out of hand.

PIPELINE:

Something, something's got to be done.

OCEANA:

Absolutely important. Safety! Safety of our precious lives and interests.

PIPELINE AND YOBE:

We know.

OCEANA:

(To YOBE.) As the appointed national authority on petroleum . . .

YOBE:

I know . . .

OCEANA:

Our deal. Remember?

YOBE:

(Patting his back.) Trust, man.

OCEANA:

I'm trying. But . . .

YOBE:

(Fist salute.) We're bound . . .

PIPELINE AND OCEANA:

(With fist salutes.) Together!

OCEANA:

(To PIPELINE.) I will always do my best. *(Pause.)* And Chief, you too . . .

PIPELINE:

Sure-sure!

YOBE:

Let's try this. Hire more guards.

OCEANA:

And Chief, be sure to tell those natives what the consequences of these riots will be. It's your responsibility. Ensure that your people are brought under control. Be firm. Tell them that violence will cost them even more than they're asking for now. We can't tolerate any irresponsible acts. Chief, control. Control your people. It's your part to play. And we'll depend . . .

(A loud explosion drowns his voice. OCEANA rises quickly, goes to fetch a large board, on which he writes: "Wanted: ONE GUARD. Qualifications: HONEST, DEPENDABLE, STRONG, HARDWORKING, MUST SPEAK ENGLISH." Trailed by the men, OCEANA now goes to mount the advertisement high up at the gate. Another loud explosion. Then they see the mob running to them from various directions. OCEANA quickly shuts the gate, and they return to their meeting.)

OCEANA:

See? See what I'm saying?

YOBE:

Who knows where they're going?

OCEANA:

But you saw them coming.

PIPELINE:

(Nudging.) Yobe, better go and see.

YOBE:

But you're their Chief . . .

OCEANA:

Yes, Chief. Go meet them.

PIPELINE:

Why me?

OCEANA:

They're your people.

YOBE:

They'll listen to you better.

PIPELINE:

These women and youths to listen? To whom?

OCEANA AND YOBE:

You, their beloved Chief.

PIPELINE:

You must be joking. Or you simply are blind to their nature. Even the blind and deaf can tell that the voices you hear out there, today's women and youths, are no longer what they used to be.

OCEANA AND YOBE:

How?

PIPELINE:

(*Emphatically.*) They don't . . . won't listen to us . . . anyone . . . Not anymore.

OCEANA:

Then get ready. They must be taught to listen. Order! Order! The rule of the law. Somebody has to be in control here. And that authority is you, Chief.

PIPELINE:

Me? But you're the Director.

OCEANA:

Oh no. Cut it out. The Government Official and I . . . We're both strangers in this land.

PIPELINE:

But he's the appointed Government Official.

OCEANA:

Yes, from the North.

YOBE:

And you from the West.

PIPELINE:

So what are both of you doing here?

YOBE AND OCEANA:

Interests . . . Others . . . ours . . .

PIPELINE:

(*Indicating YOBE.*) Oceana, yours I can understand. But Yobe, you and I are both citizens of this country. We share . . . (*Another loud explosion.*)

YOBE:

(*Impatiently.*) I know. So what do you want me to do now? Time is not on our side anymore. Tell me.

OCEANA:

First thing first. Tell them. Stop them. (*Rising.*) Teach them. Teach them to listen.

PIPELINE:

We will.

YOBE:

(*Irritated.*) We must!

OCEANA:

(*Handing* YOBE *the poster bill to mount.*) Control! Control! Control!

PIPELINE:

We'll keep on trying. (*Silence.*)

(*YOBE starts to mount the poster-ad.* OCEANA *tries to refill his pipe, but his pouch is empty. He goes into the room behind to fetch his tobacco. Rowdy chants and loud explosions tear through the smoky, humid air. The mob now swells around the locked gate. Seeing them, the Chief quickly disappears through the nearest exit. Too late;* YOBE *can go neither forward nor backward. So he retreats to join* OCEANA *at the door, where they stand watching this developing battleground. Armed with the placards and certificates, the jobless come head-on, rushing, pushing, and surging forward for positions at the gate.*)

OCEANA:

My Gaaaaad! Look. The whole damned country is at the gate. Waiting. Waiting for handouts! (*Sighs.*)

YOBE:

But it's only one job.

OCEANA:

Just one vacancy for a guard. And they're all here? The whole nation? One hundred and twenty million of them? Goooolie! These people make me sick. Sick. Sick and tired of this stinking fuc . . . (*Screaming.*) Out!
(*They ignore him and instead break into supplicating chants. "Help saar. We beg. Oga, I beg! Na beg we beg!"*)
Go away! Read the sign. One. Only one vacancy. I can't help you.
(*YOBE too adds his own threats.*)

YOBE:

Go away. The national security guards are coming!

MOB CHORUS:

Let them come. Let them come.

MOB LEADER:

Today na today-o! We dey wait.

MOB CHORUS:

(*Stomping, drumming with anything within their reach.*) Wait! Wait! We go wait! We must enter! Enter! Enter! Enter!

OCEANA:

We need guards. Guards! Security! Guards!

(*As the people chant, they ram into the gate with their bodies, hoping to force it open. The phone in the corner rings. OCEANA rushes to answer. Stunned and terrified by the news he's just heard, he drops the phone. Alarmed.*)

Gunshots?

YOBE:

Who?

OCEANA:

(*Shivering.*) My colleague.

YOBE:

Mob . . . Texac, offshore.

OCEANA:

Just narrowly escaped.

YOBE:

Again? My God! (*OCEANA nods.*)

OCEANA:

The President General has summoned us to an emergency meeting.

YOBE:

Where? When?

OCEANA:

At the headquarters. Tonight.

YOBE:

Then I must go right away.

OCEANA:

After recruiting another guard from this horde.

(*His voice is drowned by the chanting mob. "Get in line, everybody! One single file. They're coming! The Oga dey come! Yes, E dey come. I see-am! De white oga dey come. And de Government Official follow-am for back. See! See dem! And they carry gun too! Dem carry koboko," some shout. Others cry out, "Bulala! Dem carry bulala!" Panic, pandemonium ensues. Not ready for this commotion, OCEANA pulls YOBE from behind. They retreat inside to confer. Meanwhile, the mob continues their pleading and chattering outside. OMI, now masked, has joined the mob. Some of the frightened voices cry out, "So wetin? Wetin we fit do now?" Another voice responds to the question: "No? Who dey (h)ask dat kind foolish question? Wetin we fit do now? Nonsense! Dat*

no be de question for we now? We get choice. De time to do sometin is now.
No choice—no choice. We fit . . . fit do sometin. No matter how small. We fit
do sometin." Another replies: "So wetin be dat small sometin we fit do?" "Yes,
dat na de question. Dat is it! Wetin we go do, Now? Wetin be dat small tin we
go do now? E beta make we move forward and stop fighting each other. De
bigger fight dey come, sef. And if we no strong and fight together? We all go
lose. Saaam-saam!" Then others take up the refrain. "Na true. Yes. Na true
talk be dat-o! Una hear! Dem get power pass us plenty-plenty: Na true-o! Na
true-o. Dem don land-o! Make we move now! Make we act now!" Then a
screaming voice intervenes: "Dem go beat sense out of we-o! Run! Commot!
Make we run!" They panic and struggle for space as each one tries to push
and edge out the other. As the shoving and struggling continues, the one who
had raised the alarm suddenly bursts out laughing. "See them! See them!
Fools! My people dey foolish proper-proper! Na (h)only yourself you sabi
fight. Now shey una sabi fight? Fight de oga now? Where your power dey? Abi
na (h)only to knock una teet and head commot una sabi? Get ready now. Oga
dey come. Make una go knock dem teet and head commot too!" Briefly, he
breaks into mock laughter and then starts to sing a familiar tune as the oth-
ers watch in amusement.)

MAN:
They want a guard, not a nurse.

ANOTHER MAN:
They want a guard . . . a security guard.

MAN:
And that's a man's job.

WOMAN:
Guard? Who says a woman can't do that job?

WOMEN:
Who says? Who says? Just try us! Dare to try us!

WOMAN:
What a man can do?

WOMEN:
A woman can do also.

WOMAN:
Better!

WOMEN:
Better! Better! Better! Women are better! (*Chanting, dancing.*) Women
are better! Better! Better! Women are better!

MEN:
(*Shoving them aside.*) You women, give us a chance and go away.

MAN:
Or better, go find your place in the kitchen.
(*The men laugh.*)

WOMAN:
So you're men for nothing?

WOMEN:
(*Teasing.*) Our good for nothing . . .

MEN:
Shut up! Useless women!

WOMEN:
Ohoo! They like to shut us up. Go and shut the oil wells!

WOMAN:
Yes, the flaming oil well!

WOMEN:
Dripping with our blood. Yes, shut them down! Shut down the Oil Club!

WOMAN:
And dat yeye government?

WOMEN:
Stop! Stop! Stop the bloody government!

WOMAN:
With your so-called power, what can you do to the White man?

ANOTHER WOMAN:
And the Government Official?

WOMEN:
Go fight them now. Fight the Oil Club! Fight! Fight them! Fight them who are against us!

WOMAN:
(*Perhaps IMO, pushing her way through.*) Nonsense! You men should go roast in the oil fire. Yes, go fry your souls in the kitchen. OK? (*The men are protesting and trying to shout her down, but she's defiant.*) Don't you have hands to cook?

MAN:
You women of nowadays with your long tails.

ANOTHER MAN:
Only that? Long beaks!

MAN:
To suck blood! Woman sabi make plenty-plenty blood.

WOMAN:
(*Protesting.*) And you eat them?

MAN:

Blood or women?

ANOTHER MAN:

Both. What's the difference? Woman is blood. Ha! Ha! Ha!

WOMAN:

(*IMO.*) All that some of you men need is a good sharp knife to cut off those long tails of yours.

ANOTHER WOMAN:

(*Laughing.*) That should keep them quite. Cut them to size.

WOMAN:

At least for a while until they come crawling on their hands.

ANOTHER WOMAN:

Den you chop am saam-saam like rotten yam . . .

WOMAN:

To be cast off.

WOMEN:

Fit only for the garbage! Ha! Ha! Ha!

MAN:

You hear them? Bloody women!

VOICE ONE:

You too. Yeye men! That's how you people oppress us in this land just because we're . . .

VOICE TWO:

(*Loud from behind.*) Stop dis nonsense man-woman palava you all. Wetin? We dey cry here for beta tin. For we life and you just dey run your mouth like broken water pipe dey wet each other wey you all suppose to dey talk for each other. Abi? You know wetin life be? You scratch my back . . .

CHORUS:

I scratch yours.

VOICE ONE:

Na soooo!

CHORUS:

True-true!

VOICE TWO:

But that doesn't mean we won't fight for ourselves, each of us.

CHORUS:

Of course. No be why we come here?

VOICE TWO:

Yes! That's why we poor people, man or woman, must join hands together to fight our common enemies, these rich and powerful people. Haba! So make una forget wetin dey between una, man-woman and begin to dey work together for all una beta.

CHORUS:

Na true talk be dat!

VOICE ONE:

Dat no be de case. Na de problem with this country. Everybody comes last and wants to be treated first! Shame! Shame on you all! (*Spits in disgust.*)

VOICE TWO:

You know how long I've been waiting for this opportunity? (*Counting.*) One, two, three, four, five, six. Six whole months of my life just waiting to get this opportunity to be interviewed. And for what? Security guard. Yes! With a university degree.

VOICE ONE:

That's all? Six months? My friend, you just got started.

VOICE TWO:

Keep quiet, my friend! You know how long I've been waiting myself?

ANGRY VOICES:

(*Shouting.*) So, who cares? Are we not all waiting too? Are we not all in the same sinking boat?

VOICE TWO:

(*Played by OMI.*) No, my people. Some of us have paddled our canoes ashore long before and ahead of others. Yes, some of us have long been in the sea, casting our nets wide, burning the midnight oil . . . with strong faith to catch fish. And actually with a lot of struggle. We did. We thought we were loaded. (*Dips into her pocket, wields degrees.*) These! These are the fishes I caught. But can I eat them? No? I caught fishes that are not edible. They've been here, right in my net. But I can neither eat nor sell them because nobody will buy my fish. Dead. Dead. My fishes are dead. And I'm still carrying them around. Just looking . . . looking for a buyer . . . My people, what does one do with a dead fish? It stinks? Throw it back into the sea? What then will I hold onto? What if the condition improves? The tide rises high and my fish comes back alive again? But then, my net is torn, I know. What if I can't catch any more . . . ? What if? What if? My people. These are my questions to you all. Help me find answers. Pleeeeeasssseee!

(*She places her degrees at the center of the circle. Other frustrated youths join in this ritual act. Soon, they pile them up into a heap, ready to make a bonfire.*)

ANOTHER YOUNG VOICE:
And you think you're alone? Here's mine.

ANOTHER VOICE:
And mine!

ANOTHER VOICE:
Mine too.

MORE VOICES:
Mine! Mine! Mine! Mine tooooooo!

A VOICE:
What do we do with trophies without meaning?

CHORUS:
What? What do we do—what we do?

A VOICE:
(*Trying to light a match.*) Useless. They're useless.

ANOTHER VOICE:
Our education is useless. Worthless!

A VOICE:
So what do we do?

ANOTHER VOICE:
Burn them!

CHORUS:
Burn them! Burn them! (*They advance to light the bonfire.*)

BONNY/OLD MAN:
(*Blocking them.*) Stop, children! What do you think you're doing?

VOICES:
Getting rid of our load.

BONNY/OLD MAN:
And you think you can make it by burning up, destroying what you already have?

VOICES:
Yes. What's the use of keeping them when they're worthless to us?

BONNY/OLD MAN:
Your certificates? Degrees?

VOICES:
Yes. Papers! Papers! Not life. And they can burn! We can't spend our entire youth waiting.

BONNY/OLD MAN:
> (*Laughing, calming them down.*) True, I agree. It's not fair.

ANGRY VOICES:
> The system's not fair!

BONNY/OLD MAN:
> (*Still smiling.*) Children, let's talk about fairness! You know how long I've been waiting here?

VOICE ONE:
> (*Challenging.*) What? When?

BONNY/OLD MAN:
> Child, long before you and maybe your father and mother were born.

VOICE TWO:
> You too, Baba? What the hell are you doing here?

VOICE ONE:
> He's applying to be a security guard.

VOICE TWO:
> (*Laughing.*) Sure the Baba will be first.

CROWD:
> From behind. Yes! (*They burst out laughing.*)

VOICE TWO:
> Go home, old man. And rest in peace.

CROWD:
> In pieces!

BONNY/OLD MAN:
> (*Delirious.*) I blame anybody? No. It's my luck. All my life, I've been waiting. In line. I've been in this godforsaken place waiting. Hoping against hope just to get my turn. But here I am still, struggling and trying to find my way . . . my place among these young people that are not even as old as my youngest child. Is it their fault? No? But the government? This government? These rulers? Long before some of them were born, I started serving this country. Even forced to fight, for I-don't-know-who now in Burma . . . India. Yes! I did. And that was when I was still a young man. Yes, me too. Young. Young. Do they remember? Does anyone remember that now? No? But I do. (*Voice cracking.*) Yes. I spent my entire youth serving this country. And now . . .

A VOICE:
> But Baba, we the youth today are just asking, waiting for an opportunity to serve.

ANOTHER VOICE:
> Don't interrupt the old man. Let him speak!

ANOTHER VOICE:

The youths today have no respect for anybody. Old Baba, go on. Let's hear your story.

A VOICE:

His complaint!

ANGRY VOICES:

Shut up! Let the old man speak! (*Brief silence.*)

CROWD:

Yes, Baba. Speak. We're listening!

BONNY/OLD MAN:

(*Clearing his throat.*) Then I came back from the war, joined the railway company. Worked and worked until I was tired . . . with the promise that we'll all get our pension. Ask me where that pension is now? Ask, children. Where is my pension? Why am I, an old man of 65 years standing here, fighting my way with hundreds of you to interview for a security job that will only be given to one person? Just one single person . . . One single job for a whole community?

(*OCEANA and YOBE suddenly reemerge. They're heavily armed. YOBE orders 99 percent of them to step aside.*)

OSHIMI:

See? E troway me because I be woman.

BONNY/OLD MAN:

No. Na because you be old woman.

OSHIMI:

(*Vexed.*) I old pass you?

BONNY/OLD MAN:

No curse me-o.

OCEANA:

(*Angry.*) Quiet!

MOB:

(*Banging at the gate.*) Open! Open the gate!

OCEANA:

You're trespassing.

MOB:

Who?

OCEANA:

All of you. This is private property.

MOB:

In our land.

OCEANA:

(*Screaming.*) Now silence!
(*The rumbling and shoving decrease somewhat. But each one displaced is still struggling for place and prominence.*)

YOBE:

Do you hear me?

MOB:

Noooooooo! (*OCEANA and YOBE again confer and retreat into the villa.*)

YOBE:

Now silence. The Director speaks!

MOB LEADER:

Director of wetin?

A VOICE:

Director of hunger!

VOICES:

(*Chanting.*) Director of Death! Homelessness! Director of Unemployment.

MOB CHORUS:

Jobless! Jobless! Jobless!

MOB LEADER:

Director of Pollution!

MOB CHORUS:

Pollution! Pollution! Pollution! Director of pollution!

MOB LEADER:

You be de Managing Director?

MOB CHORUS:

Hear! Hear! You Damaging Director, hear! Hear! Hear! Hear. Damaging Director. Hear! Hear! Hear!
(*The displaced crowd is so enraged, they surge forward, dangerously rattling the iron gate as OCEANA and YOBE return.*)

OCEANA:

Silence!

YOBE:

And get in line.
(*They calm down, then shove and push to get in line. They all wave certificates, degrees, and whatever else they brought with them.*)

OCEANA:

(*Shouting.*) Get in line, everybody. Just a simple instruction. Get in line. Order! Nothing will be done without order!

(*As the crowd reorganizes itself,* OCEANA *again retreats with* YOBE *to plan their strategies. The people continue quarreling among themselves in the background.*)

VOICE ONE:

(*Struggling to make his way through.*) Don't push me. I came here before you.

VOICE TWO:

(*Pushing.*) Who say dat? Me, I dey wait here and wait and wait. Five years. That's how long I've been waiting to get this opportunity to stand out here in the sun and be told to shut up, instead of being given a job and allowed to work. Work! Work? Yes. I'm begging for work, not handout or charity. Look, I'm thirty-something years old. Graduated from the university five years ago and still scrambling and groping for a place . . . a job. Is that how to be a man? When? When? When will I ever be . . . become a man? Imagine the waste. Six years of my life in primary school. Five years in secondary school. Another four . . . five . . . in the university. And yet another five . . . six . . . eternal years waiting . . . waiting . . . just to be invited to an . . . and I'm not even sure of that? (*Voice cracking.*) How? (*Tearfully.*) How long? How long? (*Sighs, starts flexing his muscles.*) Look. Look at my hands. I'm able. I can work. I can dig. I can type. I can shovel. I can read. I can write . . . I can . . . I can . . . (*Voice cracking.*) How? How long? How long?

(*Sighing.* BONNY/OLD MAN *shoves himself forward and takes the center stage.*)

BONNY/OLD MAN:

Child, you ask me again? (*Silence.*) Look at me. You see my head? (*Taking off his cap and showing it to the crowd.*) Now, count. Count the gray on my head and guess how long I've been waiting? (*Silence.*) For life! (*Hysterical laughter.*) If you children are complaining about waiting for the better life? Now look who's talking? What about me?

ANOTHER VOICE:

(*Surging forward.*) What about me?

OTHER VOICES:

Wetin? What about *we*?

CHORUS:

Us?

VOICE ONE:

Go siddon! You people came late.

OLDER VOICES:

And we parents? What about the parents?

BONNY/OLD MAN:

Oh, children. You'll never know how much weighs on the back of parents!

OLDER VOICES:

We parents. Without money, without power, without without without . . .

BONNY/OLD MAN:

Yes. You feel less than a man.

OLDER WOMAN:

And as a woman?

WOMEN:

You feel less. And less. (*Mock laughter.*)

OLDER VOICE:

And what about parents?

OLDER VOICES:

You feel—you feel less. And LESS!

BONNY/OLD MAN:

Oh, children! You'll never know how we long to be men.

IMO:

(*Stepping forward.*) And women! (*Screaming.*) Hear us, you who abuse us!

ANOTHER VOICE:

And she said it!

MOB:

Hear ! Hear! Hear, you who abuse us!

YOUNGER VOICES:

What about us?

OLDER VOICES:

Time . . .

YOUNGER VOICES:

Time is us! Now!

OLDER VOICES:

And we? What do we do? What should parents do? We have no voice.

IMO:

Speak, parents! Let the parents speak!

(*The mob breaks into a chant as BONNY/OLD MAN disappears.*)

MOB:

(*Clamoring and drumming.*) Let the parents speak! Let our parents speak! Hear them—hear them—hear them speak! Hear them speak! Hear them speak!

(*In this charged and heated ground,* OCEANA *reemerges with* YOBE. *Pointing in a certain direction of the crowd, the allies confer.*)

OCEANA:
(*Nodding.*) OK. I hear.
(YOBE *sifts through the crowd and eliminates more women and the old men, whom he orders to step aside.*)

YOBE:
(*Departing.*) It's time. I've got to be at the security meeting.

OCEANA:
Hurry up now.

(*With the help of* YOBE, *the Government Official, the eliminated ones are ordered out of the premises.* OCEANA *inspects the preliminary list of candidates.* YOBE *disappears through the door behind the lounge.* BONNY/GUARD X *now quickly appears, masked, dressed in a sparkling white long-sleeve shirt, a pair of trousers, shoes, and tie to match. Reappearing as one of the candidates, he joins the queue.* OCEANA *picks him out.*)

OCEANA:
You, follow me. (BONNY/GUARD X *as job applicant obeys.* OCEANA *hands him a baton, a gun, handcuffs, and a red uniform. Protests, shouts, and more anger from those rejected.*)
You're hired. (BONNY/GUARD X *bows.*) The rest of you? Fired! (*To* BONNY/GUARD X.) Guard, get them out of here.

BONNY/GUARD X:
When you finish?

OCEANA:
Now, idiot!

BONNY/GUARD X:
(*Military salute.*) Yes saar! (*He orders them to leave, but they resist.*)

OCEANA:
Shoot any offender at sight.

BONNY/GUARD X:
(*Fidgeting.*) Ye . . . ye . . . saar!
(*In panic, he tries to pull the trigger, but he's too nervous to make an impact.* BONNY/GUARD X *begins to push them away. Another tug of war begins.*)

A VOICE:
You see? They've hired again from another tribe. But we're here. They won't employ us.

ANOTHER VOICE:
Who are we? Do we count?

VOICES:
Oga Director, is it fair? Is it fair? Right inside our own land. Right here in our own land. Oga, is it fair?

OCEANA:
(*From his distance.*) No apologies folks! Ask your government. I have a contract. It's my bargain with your government. (*Reads.*) "Hire those who would best protect your interest. For compensation, see the owners of the land." And that we have done!

A VOICE:
Na lie! They took my own land.

ANOTHER VOICE:
And drilled oil right inside my own farmland. Now I have nowhere to farm. And leveled my rubber plantation.

A VOICE:
How long? How long? (*Echoes of "how long" fill the air. The protesters still resist even as the Guard threatens to shoot at them. As they chant their protests, they form a human shield in a circle, then break into a soulful tune. The new Guard shouts his orders for them to leave, but they won't budge. OCEANA returns and orders them out, but they refuse. Instead, they begin to throw rotten tomatoes, eggs, missiles, anything they can get hold of until OCEANA retreats to the door and yells his final order.*)

OCEANA:
Shoot at sight!
(*Still in a panic, BONNY/GUARD X pulls the trigger. A young man falls. Commotion, stampede as the mob flees in different directions. Some carry the fallen shoulder-high as they sing a dirge.*)

IMO:
(*Threatening.*) We will not be silenced!

CHORUS OF VOICES:
We will retaliate!

IMO:
Oh, yes. We will.

CHORUS OF VOICES:
Retaliate! Retaliate! Retaliate! You just get ready. Ready! Ready!!

IMO:
Your people must pay.

CHORUS OF VOICES:
Pay! Pay! Pay! Their people must pay!
(*They sing, circle until blackout.*)

MOVEMENT EIGHT

(*OMI steals back into the GRA/Oil Club with her lover, IKPOBA now as Guard Y. They quickly grab Oceana's loaded briefcase, put on his coat, and go into hiding. OCEANA returns from his meeting. He is visibly agitated, smoking and pacing up and down until the YOBE, the Government Official, and PIPELINE, the Chief, arrive for their meeting. Long silence.*)

YOBE:
Tell us why you sent for us.

OCEANA:
(*Really agitated.*) To warn you . . . us . . . Things have taken a dangerous turn. Stay on high alert.

PIPELINE AND YOBE:
What? How?
(*Silence. Oceana's smoke is floating.*)

OCEANA:
Something terrible. We are losing. The profit margin is sliding down. I've just read the annual fiscal report. We made only three trillion . . .

PIPELINE:
(*Wide-eyed.*) Three what?

YOBE:
Trillion, he said.

OCEANA:
Yes. Mere three trillion. That's all we made this year. Bare. A bare market. (*Sighs.*) Tell me, what are we going to do?

PIPELINE:
With three trillion?

OCEANA:
Hey, Chief! Watch out. I'm serious. (*He steps inside.*)

YOBE:
He means business.

PIPELINE:
I see.

(*OCEANA returns with documents that he shares with his partners.*)

OCEANA:
You see? Much below expectation, at least compared to the double-digit profit for last year and also projected for this year.

PIPELINE:
Well, things do change.

OCEANA:
I know. But at whose expense? (*Silence.*) Yes, tell me. Who pays for the change? You? Me? Us?

PIPELINE AND YOBE:
(*Screams offstage.*) I guess not.

OCEANA:
Then do. Do something!

YOBE:
We have to.

OCEANA:
(*Screams offstage.*) Our investments are not safe.

PIPELINE:
And lives too!

OCEANA:
Ahaa! Now you said it! Fear . . . I'm afraid . . . (*Pauses, takes a deep breath.*) But how can anyone invest in a land that's so unstable? The primary rule of capital investment. Stability. Stability. Stability! And that's grossly lacking here. Just in the last month alone, with their riots, we've lost three million. Isn't that enough loss . . . sacrifice for us to give to this goddamn country? I mean . . . excuse my language. But I stand by the truth. And I'm really getting sick of . . . (*Makes a dash for the room again.*)

PIPELINE:
The truth?

YOBE:
The whole mess.

PIPELINE:
Country . . .

YOBE:
Your business. (*Pause.*) Why can't we agree on anything?

PIPELINE:
Our way . . . ?

YOBE:
Yes. Right! So what is new?

OCEANA:
(*Returning, stomping his cigarette.*) What is *not* new?

PIPELINE AND YOBE:
That is the question!

OCEANA:
There's always something . . . something, always. And now they have the guts to come to a director's home to rob . . .

PIPELINE:
Which?

PIPELINE AND YOBE:
(*Alarmed.*) Who dared?

OCEANA:
Who else? *Your* noble people, of course!

YOBE:
I'm so sorry about this development.

PIPELINE:
Me too.

OCEANA:
You better be. Especially you, Chief. Your people are getting quite unruly. Warn . . . restrain them. Because I won't take any shit from those blasted idiots. I too am going on the offensive.

PIPELINE:
We can . . . not . . .

OCEANA:
(*Ignores him and starts to parody the indigenous people's accent.*) "Our people are suffering—Our people are suffering . . . Suffering . . . Suffering . . . No jobs—no jobs?" Am I responsible? What is my business if they can't feed? And why should I help if all they do is spend time, valuable time, making trouble instead of money?

PIPELINE:
But how will they make money if . . .

OCEANA:
(*Furious.*) Then let them go and work. Find jobs!

PIPELINE:
But it's not that easy.

OCEANA:
Yes. Control. We've lost . . .

PIPELINE:
We're trying . . .

OCEANA:
To lose it. That's what you're doing.

PIPELINE:
No. Believe me, director. Everything's being done to . . .

OCEANA:
Liquidate us.

YOBE:
Oh, no!

PIPELINE:
Far from it, director. The people are getting only more and more agitated.

OCEANA:
(*Sarcastically.*) Any other news?

PIPELINE:
Hmm . . . well . . .

OCEANA:
Say it.

PIPELINE:
They still need . . .

OCEANA:
(*Furious.*) Jobs! Job! Jobs!

PIPELINE:
Food. Electricity! Water!

OCEANA:
Hello! The people's Solicitor and Advocate! I'm not in their way. Am I?

PIPELINE:
No . . . Who can say . . . Ehm . . . (*Coughs.*)

OCEANA:
That's the sea right there. It's completely open to them. Fish or drown—I'm not in anybody's way. Or are they claiming there's a water shortage in the sea too?

PIPELINE:

(*Fidgeting.*) Oh no. How can? Just . . . just that they can't drink sea water. Nobody does.

OCEANA:

Hey! Wait a minute, Chief. On whose side are you?

PIPELINE: ˙

Yours!

(*They laugh.*)

OCEANA:

Then maybe your people need to start importing water from abroad. After all, you import nearly everything else, even the fuel . . .

YOBE:

But that's only temporary. Our refineries have all broken down.

OCEANA:

Your excuse?

YOBE:

Importing fuel is the only option. At least for now.

OCEANA:

(*Sarcastically.*) Thanks for the information. But I must tell you. I hate people blaming others. And you people are just so good at that.

YOBE:

The simple solution is to . . .

PIPELINE:

Create more jobs.

YOBE:

And more.

OCEANA:

Did I not employ a guard only . . . ?

PIPELINE:

Well, that's just one. I mean . . . the people are suffering.

OCEANA:

(*Mock laughter.*) Their mantra! Yes, their claim to fame! Bravo! Su-ffe-ring. Su-ffe-ring! Africa's other name!

YOBE:

It doesn't take much. Just something. If only we'd appear to be doing something.

OCEANA:

If you say so.

PIPELINE:
I know my people.

OCEANA:
But do they know you?

PIPELINE:
We need to cover . . .

OCEANA:
How?

YOBE:
Our tracks. Jobs. I mean . . . (*Coughs.*)

PIPELINE:
More jobs!

OCEANA:
OK, then. What?

YOBE:
Employ more cooks, stewards, gardeners, janitors etc.

OCEANA:
That's more salaries and benefits to pay. The stake keeps getting higher
and higher every day. How are we going to pay for all that excess?

YOBE:
Hire them part-time. No . . . (*Pause.*) Still problematic. No. (*Pensive.*)
Maybe we'll just drill more oil. Sell more barrels per day. And with
some OPEC members bought . . . I mean . . . competing against each
other . . .

OCEANA:
(*Ecstatic.*) Great! Always a good idea to pump more crude. I like that.

YOBE:
Certainly means more oil glut . . . for us.

OCEANA:
Too bad. It's the price of the game. Don't take it personally. You'll make
up anyway. You both.

YOBE:
(*Winking at* OCEANA.) Well, after . . .

PIPELINE:
(*Winking at* OCEANA.) We'll talk.

OCEANA:
Still on this business, huh? (*His eyes suddenly light up as he rises.*) Yes,
I got the answer!

PIPELINE:
What?

YOBE:
Tell us!

OCEANA:
(*Grabs the map hanging by the wall. He shows it to them.*) You see this?

PIPELINE AND YOBE:
The bridge to the pipeline?

OCEANA:
It's strategic. We know that. Don't we?

PIPELINE AND YOBE:
Yes!

OCEANA:
Now. We've just built an expressway linking the inland with the off-shore line. And it's a lot of traffic. Traders traveling to buy and sell, you know?

PIPELINE AND YOBE:
Yes.

OCEANA:
OK, That's it. That's the answer! We'll just erect a toll gate here on this spot. (*Pointing.*) The junction between this "crude state" and this refinery spot. With the tolls collected from the people we can create employment for the villagers on both sides of the river and pay their salary too.

YOBE:
A great idea. Except these insatiable crooks. They'll print their own tickets anyway. Sell half for government and half for themselves.

PIPELINE:
Then collect more.

YOBE:
You'd be lucky if they give you any receipts. They'll keep telling motorists that they've run out of receipts. So what do we do?

OCEANA:
Then don't pay the damn . . . Don't take it. No pay without receipts!

PIPELINE:
(*Laughing.*) My friend, you really don't know how the system works. "No business, no show."

YOBE:
As the girls say nowadays. Money for hand, back na ground!

PIPELINE:

"No honey, no money!" I've heard that too. (*They laugh.*)

YOBE:

Seriously, it sounds like a good idea.

OCEANA:

And more. We have better security. A new checkpoint will be added.

PIPELINE:

And a canteen too, where the workers can eat.

YOBE:

And the women can find jobs as cooks. I personally would need cleaners, janitors.

PIPELINE:

Me too. I'll need more domestic help.

OCEANA:

Sure. Our pets are lonely . . . just too lonely. You know, Dr. Vet recently made a major discovery . . . (*Pause.*) That Hero . . . my Hero . . . is suffering from depression.

YOBE:

Your dog, too?

OCEANA:

Yes. Poor thing. Abused. Abused. We must protect their rights.

PIPELINE:

Animals . . .

OCEANA:

Precious pe . . . Handle with care. Your people better be warned. I'll kill for my pet. Your people better be warned. Handle with care. (*Excited as he sells the idea now.*) Pets. Dogs . . . man's very best friend. Trust them. Train them as security guards. Much more reliable, I tell yeah. Give them a clinic too. You know this year alone, many have died from cholera? No clean water.

PIPELINE:

Too bad for them . . .

OCEANA:

(*Fiercely.*) For us!

PIPELINE:

I have a great idea.

YOBE:

Build industries to create jobs.

OCEANA:
Nonsense!

YOBE:
Far too expens . . .

OCEANA:
Expensive, yes! And who's to pay for all that?

PIPELINE:
Who else but you . . .

OCEANA:
Don't be silly, Chief. You mean I came here to serve . . . (*Rising with a spark in his eyes.*) Look, gentlemen. You know what? I've got the solution. (*The others listen attentively.*) A great idea. Your people would be better served if we had a nursery.

PIPELINE AND YOBE:
Oh yes, a nursery! Their children . . .

OCEANA:
Our dogs!

PIPELINE:
(*Alarmed.*) What?

OCEANA:
Our pets are suffering. Cabin fever. We work too hard. Too long and not enough time to give them quality care. And these pets are really the only true friends . . . companions that we have in the field. (*Pause.*) We need to protect our own. Build a nursery for them.

PIPELINE:
Yes, but . . .

OCEANA:
Just listen to me. A pet house will cost much less.

PIPELINE:
(*Laughing.*) Oh yes. Rather reminds me of a joke I heard from a friend about an African woman who was trying to rent a house in America. The landlord required that she fill out long forms to prove herself, her assets, her credit worthiness and all that. And you know those Americans? Just as we do . . . I tell you, those people don't joke with their penny. Money? *Their* life. Ha! (*Bucolic laughter.*)

YOBE:
So what happened to the African woman?

PIPELINE:
My friend said that everything was OK until she was about to append her signature to the lease and then the Landlord asked, "By the way,

Miss, do you have kids?" And thinking that her children were her great assets, the woman proudly relied, "Oh yes. Four. I'm blessed with four children." Immediately, the Landlord's face turned red. He rose, tore up the lease and showed the woman to the door. "Sorry, ma'am. I can't rent my house to you. Pets OK. No kids." "Wh . . . wha . . . What," the stunned woman managed to cry out. "I repeat. Pets OK. No kids! Goodbye!" The landlord slammed the door in her face.

OCEANA:
And that's right.

PIPELINE:
Who?

YOBE:
(*Chuckling.*) Let's face it . . .

OCEANA:
(*Ignoring them.*) I know a good vet-doctor in Texas. Hire him.

YOBE:
But we still need something . . . Something more . . .

PIPELINE:
Like a general hospital for the people?

OCEANA:
We can't afford it.

PIPELINE:
But we afford one for dogs?

OCEANA:
(*Furious.*) Yes, sir! Who's going to pay for a general hospital? You'll need to hire more specialized professional staff, fringe benefits, doctors, nurses, lab technicians, aides, and more.

YOBE:
(*Drinking.*) I see. The more skilled workers, the higher the salary. Benefits. Retirement benefits. Worker's compensation. Housing. It's true. We can't afford it now. (*PIPELINE turns away in silence.*)

OCEANA:
Great! Great reasoning, my friend! The less committed we are to these people, the better. So I propose that all future employment that we offer be part-time. Temporary. Gives us the flexibility and controlling edge. (*To PIPELINE.*) Your silence troubles . . . I mean, are you with me?

PIPELINE:
(*Startled.*) Oh, yes. Too much with you. Just thinking . . .

OCEANA:

(*Calmly.*) What now, Chief?

PIPELINE:

(*Winking at OCEANA.*) You and I can make . . . make a deal . . . I mean ehmm . . . work together.

OCEANA:

Of course! Of course! (*Silence as YOBE tries to make the rest of the deal with his eyes.*) Produce more jobs. There's more than enough care to go around. You agree?

YOBE:

Sure! Some will walk the dogs in the morning. Others will have to walk them in the evening.

PIPELINE:

Hmm . . . But a full-time job just for dog care? People are going to think it's insulting.

OCEANA:

(*Chuckling.*) As if they're any better!

YOBE:

We'll stress that we need those dogs for security.

OCEANA:

(*Fist salute.*) Thanks. Friends, thank you! And the sooner, the better.

PIPELINE:

(*Looks at his partners.*) So it's a deal?

YOBE:

If *we* say so.

OCEANA:

And it is!

YOBE:

(*Smacking his lips, saluting PIPELINE playfully.*) Man no die!

PIPELINE:

Man no rotten!

YOBE:

Do we have a choice?

PIPELINE:

I guess not.

YOBE:

We're together.

PIPELINE:

(*Winking at him.*) Till *they* do us part! (*They all laugh.*)

OCEANA:

(*Drinks, seals the deal.*) We'll start immediately. And the pet nursery shall be called, "The New Haven."

PIPELINE:

The holy place?

OCEANA:

Yes. Most sacred.

YOBE:

A New Haven for dogs and cats?

OCEANA:

Sure. Now you're talking! Gentlemen, let's drink to that! (*Toasts.*) (*They all laugh. PIPELINE rises, winks again at OCEANA.*)

PIPELINE:

Our deal.

OCEANA:

My seal.

YOBE:

It's time.

PIPELINE:

(*Leaving.*) We'll see later then.

(*Exit PIPELINE. OCEANA disappears behind the door, returns with a sign, which he hands over to YOBE to put up. Suddenly, the masked youths emerge from their hiding and leap into the space. In panic, OCEANA fires at the nearest one. Omi's lover, IKPOBA, falls, injured. OMI flees. Lights fade out on OCEANA as he stares at the wounded youth, who's pleading for help and life. "Don't kill me. Please! Please!" Finally, OCEANA stoops, starts dragging the wounded boy away until lights fade out. Flute sounds in the background.*)

MOVEMENT NINE

(It's twilight. IMO is in the Market-Square, chanting invocations to her ancestors to rise up and come to their aid.)

IMO:

Rise up, mothers! My ancestors. Wake! Wake. Wake up! Your daughters need you now. The tide is high, high up. The flood threatens to swallow us. And sharks, white and black, have taken over the shores. Our land. Arise mothers! Your daughters are sinking. Drowning. Gobbled as torn flesh by the ever hungry sharks now ruling our land. *(Desperately.)* Can't you hear me? Mothers, arise! Lead us!

(She's crying so loud, the other women and youths are alarmed and begin to arrive at the Market-Square. They declare a Town Meeting. OSHIMI rouses and addresses the gathering.)

OSHIMI:

Mothers, sons, and daughters. Who owns this land?

CHORUS:

We own the land!

OSHIMI:

I say who owns this land?

CHORUS:

We own the land!

OSHIMI:

I say who?

CHORUS:

We!

OSHIMI:

Who?

CHORUS:

We!

(With all of them now completely animated, OSHIMI clears her throat to speak.)

OSHIMI:

Mothers, sons, and daughters of the land. It is I, Oshimi. The umbilical cord, running all through these coasts from here to the Fouta Djallon mountain that speaks. You know me, I know you. I, Oshimi, leader of the marketplace, appointed by you, women of this land, to lead you with the assistance of sister Cross River. But this is not about me . . . or her. It is about us . . . us. Our world! Women of Sufferland, you appointed us to serve you. We are here, ready. My siblings from many shores. Today, I speak to you, not about anything new or events that you're not familiar with. Something . . . something strange, smelly, and strong is sapping our land. Why? Why? Why? Has it always been so? What is happening to our . . . world . . . our land?

(She's choking. Those nearest to her hold her from falling. As she recovers, CROSS RIVER rises and takes over.)

CROSS RIVER:

You heard her, our sister. She said it! What did mama say?

CHORUS OF WOMEN:

Something. Strange. Smelly. Strong is sapping our land.

CROSS RIVER:

People of the land and sea. I know we all have come from different directions to meet here. We are here, now. Together. What are we going to do? As they say, if you don't lick and massage your lips, the dry fierce harmattan wind will lick it for you. People of Sufferland! Our land bleeds! The land weeps! Tell me, who among you here, no matter how young, no matter how old, has not lost our blood?

CHORUS OF WOMEN:

All! All of us!

CROSS RIVER:

Your fathers and brothers?

CHORUS OF WOMEN:

Lost, branded, or wounded!

CROSS RIVER:

Your mothers and sisters?

CHORUS OF WOMEN:

(Inflamed.) Defied, maimed, or murdered!

CROSS RIVER:

Your pride and dignity?

CHORUS OF WOMEN:

Cut down!

CROSS RIVER:

And if they take all that away, what then is left?

CHORUS OF WOMEN:
Nothing! Nothing!

CROSS RIVER:
Not even the land is left. Not taken. Not polluted.

CHORUS OF WOMEN:
Nothing! Nothing!

CROSS RIVER:
We're taken.

CHORUS OF WOMEN:
Taken. Taken. Taken!

CROSS RIVER:
Ever since they discovered oil in our land, they drill, dry, and fry us alive with the fishes and farmlands all cooking in the oil.

CHORUS OF WOMEN:
The oil. Our oil!

CROSS RIVER:
So what will become of us . . . our children? (*Pause.*) Do you smell the decaying bodies of husbands, sons, and daughters?

CHORUS OF WOMEN:
Yes!

CROSS RIVER:
Do you smell the fishes roasting in their hot oil poured over the rivers?

CHORUS OF WOMEN:
Yes! They've refined our oil into a curse!

CROSS RIVER:
Where? Where else in the world does oil cease to anoint?

CHORUS OF WOMEN:
Here! Here! Here!

CROSS RIVER:
Plants, animals, children, men, women cooking in their oil. Oil sapped from the very soul of our sagging land. Ah! People of Sufferland! Do you see yourselves drowning?

CHORUS OF WOMEN:
Yes!

CROSS RIVER:
Starving?

CHORUS OF WOMEN:
Yes!

CROSS RIVER:
Wilting?

CHORUS OF WOMEN:
Yes!

CROSS RIVER:
What then are you waiting for, mothers, sons, and daughters?
(*In this fury, the mob rises, facing the direction of the GRA/Oil Club.*)

CHORUS OF WOMEN:
Nothing! Nothing! No more waiting!

CROSS RIVER:
I do not wish to speak for you or for anybody. Let every woman speak for herself. And in the end tell us women, what are we going to do (*Chanting.*) What are we going to do—what are we going to do—to do—to do—to doooo?

HADEJA:
When our land is burnt and bonded.

IMO:
Why should you when you have your army to fight your wars?

HADEJA:
Why should you stand still, your voices choking when you are the oil and the river?

IMO:
When you are the heart and breast of the land?

CHORUS:
Yes! Yes! She said it! Said it! Yes she said it!

IMO:
Why? Why? Why, mothers, sons, and daughters of Sufferland?

CHORUS:
Why-why-why?

IMO:
Who can silence the drums? Sufferland women speak!

CHORUS:
Yes! Here we are. Ready!
(*IMO breaks into military steps. They follow as they sing and dance in circles: "Onye Akpana nwa gụ aka."*)

OSHIMI:
Onye Akpana Nwagụ aka nọdụ

CHORUS OF WOMEN:
M'Ọdin ndụ. Ọnwu la nwụ!

OSHIMI:

Onye Akapana Nwagu Akano du.

CHORUS OF WOMEN:

M'Odin ndu. M'Onwu la Nwu!

OSHIMI:

Onye Akpana, Nwa gu aka nodu.

CHORUS OF WOMEN:

M' odi ndu. Onwu la nwu!
(*The women have risen into this frenzied dance, when suddenly, OMI appears in a white shroud.*)

IMO:

(*Excitedly.*) Look who's here!
(*Sudden hush.*)

OSHIMI:

(*Breathless.*) My child! My life! (*Grips OMI.*)

IMO:

Where have you been? (*All the women surround OMI, who is still panting.*)

OSHIMI:

So you are alive, my daughter?

OMI:

(*Panting.*) Ye . . . ye . . . Yes. But . . .

CROSS RIVER:

Tell us what happened? Where is my son?

OMI:

They . . . got . . . got . . . Took him.

CROSS RIVER:

(*Alarmed.*) Dead?

OMI:

Alive. But captive.

CROSS RIVER:

(*Frantic.*) Where? Tell . . . tell me . . . us!

OMI:

In jail. Their cell. But he'll return. He's strong. And he tells me to tell you not to give up. You must continue to fight. Fight! (*Still gasping.*) The ba . . . battle has just . . . just . . . begun. Mothers get ready! Sisters get ready.

IMO:

What did she say?

CHORUS OF WOMEN:
Mothers. Sisters. Get ready! Ready! Ready!

HADEJA:
And she said it!

CHORUS OF WOMEN:
Get ready! Ready! Ready!

OMI:
Are you ready?

CHORUS OF WOMEN:
Yes!
(*They start pulling off their headwraps to reinforce the wrappers around their waists. They grab stumps and broken branches and twigs. Suddenly, OMI bursts into laughter, as she watches the women. Shocked, they freeze.*)

OMI:
(*Still laughing.*) Mothers and sisters. You're not going to fight men with guns and bullets with your bare hands and twigs? (*Still frozen, the women look from one to the other.*). No, mothers and sisters. We cannot. Must not play their bloody game. For that is what they are. BLOODY!

CROSS RIVER:
So, daughter, tell us, how should we fight?

CHORUS OF WOMEN:
How? How are we going to fight their guns?

IMO:
Our souls. United . . .

HADEJA:
Again she said it!

CHORUS OF WOMEN:
Our souls! Our spirits! Fight! Fight!

OMI:
(*Rousing them.*) Wounded or healed?

CHORUS OF WOMEN:
Fight! Fight! We'll fight!

(*They chant until IMO drowns their voices with the vibrant drums of the congo music that she plays to electrify the crowd. As if called to action, their feet step up. They hold each other and break up into two concentric circles; the daughters on the one hand, and the mothers on the other. OMI now leads the daughters, while OSHIMI leads the mothers until the circles merge into one.*)

Then OMI halts them all as she unfolds to them the secret plans she's heard from the Oil Club.)

OMI:

I know the white oil director. He's planning to go on leave to America. They go every ten weeks, you know. There they spend five weeks to recover from the abuse of the weather in Africa, they say. (*Chuckles.*)

OSHIMI:

Running? Let them!

CHORUS OF WOMEN:

Just wait. Wait. Our daughters are coming!

OMI:

(*Turning to her mother.*) Mother, I'm sorry I didn't listen to you. But I'm glad, too, because by not obeying you, I too have learned. Now I know better. Forgive, forgive, mothers and sisters.
(*They embrace each other. The women break into song and serenade, until OMI again intervenes.*)
Mothers and daughters of Sufferland!

CHORUS OF WOMEN:

Eeeih!

OMI:

I get tori.
(*Immediately, the women rally round her in a half-moon shape as she declares: "Story-story?"*)

CHORUS OF WOMEN:

"Story!"

OMI:

Mothers and daughters of Sufferland. Open your eyes and ears. Get ready. The thing we have been looking for in Sokoto, we now find in our *shokoto*!

CHORUS OF WOMEN:

(*Excitedly.*) Go on! Tell us! Show us! We are ready!

OMI:

(*Smiles, confides in them.*) You know wetin?

CHORUS:

No!

OMI:

I heard many things in our hideout. After our beloved was shot and taken away, I had no way to escape. And with White man threatening with his gun, ready to shoot anyone point blank, I got scared. Very scared, and crept under those big chairs they sit on to drink whisky and brandy in their club. Then the Chief, and later the Government Official, came to see the White man to plan as usual (*Pause.*) My mothers and sisters, if you know what these people think? What they're planning for us? You'll weep.

CHORUS OF WOMEN:
Say it!

CROSS RIVER:
Dead body no be new tin for ground. Tell us!

OMI:
You really want to know?

CHORUS OF WOMEN:
Yes!

OMI:
Then get ready.

CHORUS OF WOMEN:
We are.

OMI:
Now hear it. They're putting a toll gate on that bridge linking our land across the rivers. (*Awaits their reaction.*)

OSHIMI:
And so?

CROSS RIVER:
Yes! You know. They're always mounting walls, roads, and bridges.

IMO:
Not for our own development but for moving their oil and goods from our land overseas. So it's just another bridge from our land to their pockets.

OSHIMI:
And that brings me to my question. What is in this for us?

CHORUS OF WOMEN:
Yes. What is in it for us?

OMI:
(*Smiling.*) Now listen. They say they will employ our people to collect money at the toll gate.

CHORUS OF WOMEN:
Good! Now they're talking. There will be free flow of money in our hands!

OMI:
And you know that road is so busy?

CHORUS OF WOMEN:
Yes!

CROSS RIVER:
But the tickets sold belong to them.

OMI:
Are we going to be fools forever?

CHORUS OF WOMEN:
Nooooo!

OMI:
Are we going to be used forever?

CHORUS OF WOMEN:
No! No! No!

IMO:
How monkey go dey work-work-work and baboon go dey chop?

CHORUS OF WOMEN:
No more! Who born monkey?

OMI:
No! Dem never born am!

CROSS RIVER:
We don tire for dem monkey business.

HADEJA:
She said it!

CHORUS OF WOMEN:
We tire! Tire! We don tire!

OMI:
So?

IMO:
We too go begin sell our own tickets!

CROSS RIVER:
"Shikena," as our northern brothers and sisters say.

CHORUS OF WOMEN:
That's it. So be it!

OMI AND IMO:
Who owns this land after all?

CHORUS OF WOMEN:

We! We! Our land! We must-must take back what is ours! (*Chanting.*)
Resource Control! Resource Control!

OMI:

(*Singsong manner.*) And that is just the beginning. Something, some-thing else is going to happen.

CHORUS OF WOMEN:

Tell us! Tell us daughter, tell us!

OMI:

(*Smiles mischievously, then screams.*) Mothers and daughters of Sufferland!

CHORUS OF WOMEN:

Eeih!

OMI:

Your leaders . . .

CHORUS OF WOMEN:

We have no leaders. Away with leaders!

IMO:

We're tired of being misled.

HADEJA:

(*Stepping forward.*) By the nose?

CHORUS OF WOMEN:

Enough! We reject all leaders of falsehood. We reject leaders that take and take and never give anything good in return. Away! Away with their lies!

OSHIMI:

But caution, children.

CROSS RIVER:

Yes, easy.

OSHIMI:

As our people say, "There will be enough sleep for the dead in the grave."

CROSS RIVER:

That is if they let you die in peace.

OSHIMI:

And even when you die, will they let you be buried? Sleep? That is the question! Some of us are worth more dead than alive . . .

IMO:

Buried alive.

OSHIMI:

Some of us are worth nothing dead or alive!

IMO:

That too must end. Trust us, mothers. Times are changing. We your daughters are here.

OSHIMI:

She said it! Said it!

CHORUS OF MOTHERS:

Our daughters are here! Speak! Speak daughters!
(*OMI steps forward again to the center.*)

OMI:

Now the big news!

CHORUS OF WOMEN:

We can't wait. We'll show them! We can't wait!

OMI:

Now hear what our mis-leaders are saying.

CHORUS:

We're all ears.

OMI:

Tomorrow, they're converting the Boys Quarters in their Club into a nursery daycare center.

CHORUS OF WOMEN:

For whom?

OSHIMI:

Their children of course!

OMI:

(*Smiling.*) No, Mother. For their dogs!

CHORUS OF WOMEN:

(*Stunned.*) Dogs?

OMI:

Yes. A daycare nursery for their pets and puppies.

IMO:

(*Carrying an imaginary banner.*) Welcome to the nursery. Pets, OK. No kids!

CHORUS OF WOMEN:

Ha! Ha! Ha!

OMI:

(*Carrying an imaginary microphone.*) You got insurance?

CHORUS OF WOMEN:
For dogs and puppies! (*They laugh.*) So what else?

IMO:
What else is new in this, their new world order?

OSHIMI:
What else is in it for us?

CROSS RIVER:
That is what we want to know.

CHORUS OF WOMEN:
Tell us! Tells us!

OMI:
You know, last time that Oyibo Shell director traveled home on leave? He came back and complained bitterly that his pet dog looked emaciated and emotionally disturbed because of loneliness and lack of care. His colleague, the other oil director from . . . you-know-what . . . ?

CHORUS OF WOMEN:
Yes.

OMI:
Well, he too was very bitter about his lady cat's condition. The cat had littered four kittens while he was drilling onshore . . . offshore post. He complained that his beloved lady cat and kittens were so badly neglected. He'll never forgive his housekeeper. So he fired him. And now his friend, I know only too well, vows he won't take it lying down. He's taken his "Hero."

CROSS RIVER:
Whose hero?

OSHIMI:
The dog. His Hero. Listen!

CROSS RIVER:
I see.

OMI:
Mother, you never see. The director has since entrusted that dog to a psychiatrist who said the dog was suffering from acute depression. So to heal their guilt and anger, the oil directors, with Yobe, the Government Official, have met and now want to take serious action to protect their beloved pets against such habitual abuse and negligence. So now they're renovating the recreation area in the GRA/Oil Club. The place will be well furnished and maintained as a daycare center for their ani-

mal pets. Mothers and sisters! You should see the clothes, toys, and food these strange people use to feed their animal pets! (*Showing.*) And they kiss the animal mouth-to-mouth.

OSHIMI:

Our eyes will not see corruption!

CHORUS OF WOMEN:

Abomination! Abomination! Abomination! They oppress us with their pet animals.

IMO:

They hate us and love their beloved beasts!

OMI:

Mothers and sisters. The time has come.

IMO:

We hear you.

HADEJA:

And she said it!

CHORUS OF WOMEN:

The time has come!

OMI:

If there is something I've learned by hanging around these people, it's what is of most and least value to them. One thing I know, they love their money. And pets in that order.

OSHIMI:

Those "hell" people.

OMI:

Shell, Mother?

IMO:

I saw that in their own country. They'll sure kill for anything they love.

OSHIMI:

Now what about us?

OMI AND IMO:

Ha! Ha! Ha! You and me?

CHORUS OF WOMEN:

Yes! What about us? What do we mean to those people?

HADEJA AND OMI:

Nothing. Nothing. We don't count.

IMO:

And what about our own people in government?

OMI AND HADEJA:

Ha! We don't count. Except when they want to use us.

IMO:

First we'll deal with their hearts. I mean pets.

CROSS RIVER:

(*Lighting up.*) Yom-yom! Delicious 404!! We'll make soup with their dogs.

CHORUS OF WOMEN:

Yes! Yes! Kill hunger!

(*They start drumming. The police appear at a distance and lay in ambush.*)

No more hunger!

CROSS RIVER:

A full soup-pot!

OSHIMI:

(*Smacking her lips.*) My soup will be sweet. Oh so sweet. They'll smell it right from their hell camp!

IMO:

Suya! Suya-steak! Dog meat for steak! (*They break into song and dance.*)

HADEJA:

(*Interrupting them.*) And if we deal with the foreigners, what do we do to our own?

OMI:

Those too!

CHORUS OF WOMEN:

Yes, together.

IMO:

To subdue our enemies. We must learn their own art. Go under. Know their secrets. And then act when they least expect it.

CHORUS OF WOMEN:

Yes! Yes! Their own art. Act when they least expect it. (*OMI empties the contents of the stolen briefcase.*) Here, mothers!

OMI:

The most important weapons we need is not guns but knowledge.

IMO:

Yes, wisdom.

OMI:

The weapon to conquer our enemies. We must go under.

IMO:

Know their secrets.

OMI:

Then act when they least expect.

CHORUS OF WOMEN:

Yes! Yes! We must act. Act! Act! Act!

CROSS RIVER:

But there's no time.

IMO:

Let's go!

OSHIMI:

I will be their nurse!

CROSS RIVER:

And I, their cleaner.

OMI:

But then it's underlined. The applicant must be young. Must speak good English. And must be clean. Always. Mother, how are you going to do it? You can't speak English.

HADEJA:

We'll make them over. Come mothers, let's make you up!

OSHIMI:

I'm ready and willing to learn. Nothing is impossible. Isn't that what our mothers taught us? Yes daughters, teach me.

CROSS RIVER:

Teach us daughters. We're ready. Ready! Ready to learn. That's what the time calls for. Parents, teach your children. Children, teach your parents!

CHORUS OF DAUGHTERS:

She said it! Said it!

OSHIMI:

Now show me.

(*They demonstrate and play-act as the women are made over.*)

OMI:

When you come in, you put on your apron and say (*in an affected oily tone*), "Good Day, my Director! What would you like for breakfast today?"

IMO:

> "Yes, good . . . Hannah." (*Play-acting.*) Sausage and bacon with continental breakfast please? OK?

OSHIMI:

> (*Interrupting.*) Saucer . . . and baker . . . ?

IMO:

> You know, like hot dog?

OMI:

> Oh, yes! Oh, yes, massaar. Sweet *hot dog,*! I can do it . . . I know!

IMO:

> Yes. Wash it well. Then roll it up.

OMI:

> Good, massaar. And . . . your egg? Lay it how?

IMO:

> What? Lay eggs? I don't!

OMI:

> No, saar. I mean how do you like it? Sunny side up?

IMO:

> What, massar?

OMI:

> I mean the tin . . . Your tin, saar. Like it scrambled? Or fried?

IMO:

> Oh yes, Dog. I mean, *God.* My mind . . . brain . . . A little distracted this morning. Just go ahead and boil it . . .

OMI:

> (*Smiling.*) Good, massar. I will boil it in no time at all. Thank you, saar! Thank you, saar!

IMO:

> Thank *you*! (*The women burst into laughter.*)

OMI:

> And then the rest of the ads. We want a cook for the animal daycare center.

IMO:

> I!

OMI:

> A nurse for the animal daycare . . .

HADEJA:

> I!

CROSS RIVER:
And the money collector at the toll gate?

OMI:
I guess I'm the only one left. I'll do it.

IMO:
But remember. Each one for us all.

CHORUS OF WOMEN:
Each one for everyone.

OSHIMI:
They will see not us but our handiwork.

CHORUS OF WOMEN:
Yes! Yes! Yes! They'll feel our mighty hands.

OMI:
Come mothers and sisters. I know the way. We've waited too long. It's our time. Now.

CHORUS OF DAUGHTERS:
Mothers. Sisters. Our time. Now!

CHORUS OF MOTHERS:
Lead, daughters. Lead the way. Lead us! Lead us!
(*As they march forward, their voices swell in unison as they prepare for action.*)

IMO:
Win or lose?

OSHIMI AND CROSS RIVER:
We are ready!

CHORUS OF WOMEN:
Together.

OSHIMI AND CROSS RIVER:
(*Rousing them.*) Mothers and daughters of Sufferland!

CHORUS OF WOMEN:
Eeeih!

OSHIMI:
Who owns this land?

CHORUS OF WOMEN:
We own this land!

OSHIMI:
Then take. Take back what is yours, women.

(The women drum and dance. Suddenly, siren sounds. The Police in camouflage uniform swoop on them and handcuff OSHIMI and CROSS RIVER. The women struggle to be free, even as they're being chained. Everything happens so fast. The music and dance stop abruptly. Silence. A deafening call from IMO, the women charge at the predators. The struggle intensifies. The armed men throw tear gas into the crowd. The captives are led away. But soon the mob recovers; the girls first. They rouse the women once again.)

IMO:
Is this the end of our journey?

CHORUS OF WOMEN:
(Thundering.) Noooooooooooooo!

OMI:
Where is their nursery?

CHORUS OF WOMEN:
There! In the Oil Club! *(OMI leads them now.)*

IMO:
Who lives there?

CHORUS OF WOMEN:
Dogs and cats!

HADEJA:
Do they live for us to die?

CHORUS OF WOMEN:
Noooooooooo!

OMI:
Then it's time for us to live!

CHORUS OF WOMEN:
(Marching.) It's time! Time! Time!

(Led by OMI, their voices rise in song once again as they quickly march in the direction of the GRA/Oil Club. The air is soon filled with the noises/sounds of frightened animals, followed by crashing sounds, dogs barking, a clap of thunder, with lightning flashes. Blackout.)

MOVEMENT TEN

(Back in the GRA/Oil Club. OCEANA is extremely angry. He's pacing up and down the lounge and the gate area when PIPELINE, the Chief, arrives for another emergency meeting.)

OCEANA:
No, I can't take it anymore. Find out. Find out who did it.

PIPELINE:
Did what?

OCEANA:
My cutie. My Baby Hero. Gone! *(Sighs.)*

PIPELINE:
Oh, well. Thank God it's not any human . . . I mean they didn't kill any-body. Just the dog. They probably ate . . .

OCEANA:
(Screaming.) Stop! Stop! You Thief . . . I mean, Chief. Can't you, can't you see the dog is my wife . . . I mean life. Dammit! *(Silence.)*

PIPELINE:
Oh, I'm so sorry.

OCEANA:
(Explodes.) I don't need your sorrows! Just get them! Get those culprits. Bring them to their knees! *(Fiercely.)* And especially you, Chief . . . ?

PIPELINE:
What do you want? What can I do now?

OCEANA:
Find out. They're your people. Nobody comes from another village to commit such atrocities.

PIPELINE:
Director, I want to do everything possible. But I must tell you this . . . Remember those people you have hired from outside this region?

OCEANA:

Yes. I am the Director, remember? My discretion. And I take no orders from anybody. Not even you, Chief Pipeline!

PIPELINE:

You're right, Director. But know this. You're . . . I mean, they're here, in our land. That makes all the difference. I've told you time and time again, the people are angry.

OCEANA:

Is that news?

PIPELINE:

They feel like outsiders. Marginalized. And denied in their own land.

OCEANA:

(*Angrily.*) Blast your fucking land. Everyone! Everything! To hell with . . .

PIPELINE:

Shell, my director . . . pardon. I know. What they do is pour oil and petrol on fire. But our business concern . . . you and me . . . should always be to solve these problems and remain constructive.

OCEANA:

Just don't go there. Enough! I'm not ready for any argument now. Go! All I want is to see anyone involved in this brutal murder brought to terminal justice. Don't delay. Go!

PIPELINE:

Take heart. Soon, the matter will be resolved. (*Exit PIPELINE.*)

OCEANA:

(*Alone.*) What the hell am I doing in this godforsaken land? (*He grabs his suit and bowler hat, stares, throws them to the floor.*) Go . . . go back to Tex . . . ? Oh, no. Forget it. The oil . . . oil . . . No. I can't . . . Not now . . . not now . . . The oil. The Capital. The stakes so high. Oh, so high. We'll be the losers. Oh, damn the profit! I'm frying . . . trying in the sizzling hot oil . . .
(*OCEANA is still agonizing when PIPELINE returns to announce that the culprits have been found and arrested.*)

PIPELINE:

(*Excitedly.*) We've got them. Yes! The Government Official said . . .

OCEANA:

Great! Son'v-a-b . . .

PIPELINE:

Let's drink to that.
(*OCEANA opens a bottle of whiskey, drinks.*)
At least now the ground is cleared for you to take that girl.

OCEANA:
> You got her?

PIPELINE:
> Oh, yes. How soon do you need her . . . want her to come?

OCEANA:
> Not now. Wait. Everything now has to wait. I'm tired. Tired and fed up. (*Slumps into a chairs. Sighs.*) God! Can I last one more day?

PIPELINE:
> Just trust us. Things are not as bad as you think. In fact, everything is under control.

OCEANA:
> Alarm, you mean? Whose . . .

PIPELINE:
> Oh, come on, Director. Be optimistic.
> (*Explosive noise is heard. They listen.*)

OCEANA:
> I'll blow up anybody's brain if they mess with me.

PIPELINE:
> (*Trembling.*) No. Nobody's going to . . . to . . . mess . . . mess . . . (*Another explosion.*)

OCEANA:
> (*Nervous.*) They dare not.
> (*PIPELINE is terrified but continues to pretend and peep through the gate when YOBE, the Government Offical, arrives.*)

YOBE:
> We're in deep . . . deep . . .

PIPELINE:
> Trouble? (*YOBE, too, is trembling.*)

OCEANA:
> What now?

YOBE:
> Ehm . . . Oh, God! (*Silence.*)

PIPELINE:
> Say. What's God's . . . matter, I mean . . . ?
> (*Slow drumbeats outside.*)

YOBE:
> The Texac . . . Vice . . . Deputy . . .

OCEANA:
> Killed?

YOBE:

Kidnapped!

OCEANA:

(*Hysterical.*) I knew it! I knew it! Yes! Get me out of here. Now! (*He starts packing, yells.*) Guaaarrrrd!

IKPOBA:

(*Entering as Guard Y, salutes.*) Yesssaaar!

OCEANA:

What the hell is going on there?

IKPOBA:

(*Enters, trembling.*) Hell . . . Oga! Sh . . . Shell . . . Drum . . . !

OCEANA:

(*Shaking him up*) Speak! Say what? What's going on?

IKPOBA:

Not . . . Notin . . . Notin oga!

OCEANA:

Then what's all that noise outside?

IKPOBA:

Oga no be me. Na de village people. Dem burn de (h)oil . . . de (h)oil dey for fire.

PIPELINE:

(*Alarmed.*) What?

OCEANA:

What's he babbling?

YOBE:

He means . . . he means the oil . . .

PIPELINE:

The pipeline's on fire.

OCEANA:

(*Stunned.*) What? I'll be damned! (*Silence.*)

PIPELINE:

I told you. Those people are serious.

OCEANA:

No! Savages! Good-for-nothing vandals . . . Cursed! Forever cursed! (*He throws his bunch of keys on the floor. The Guard picks them up and stands at attention while his master runs into the chamber to arm himself.*)

PIPELINE:

(*Talking to himself.*) Terrible . . . Terrible development.

YOBE:

I told you. These people are going to be our ruin.

PIPELINE:

Arrest the situation?

YOBE:

The people, you mean?

PIPELINE:

It's time. I'm going. (*Exit PIPELINE.*)

OCEANA:

(*Returns, combat-ready.*) Details. Details! Tell me who are these terrorists? How do we find them? Where?

IKPOBA:

(*Demonstrating.*) Oga, I don talk am. De people dey mad. Dem pour petrol for de place. Bring marches. De tin catch fire. Vaaaaam! Na so. No waste time. At all-at all! E dey burn like . . . like hell . . .

OCEANA:

(*Smoking, pacing up and down.*) Fire! Oh God . . . My vice . . . Protect . . . (*Sighs.*) So who's responsible? Who?

YOBE:

What a waste!

OCEANA:

What a loss! I better warn the other direct . . .
(*He grabs the phone and dials.*)

YOBE:

Who?

OCEANA:

(*Ignoring him.*) Hello! Hello! Here! The Director of Sh . . . (*He realizes that the phone is silent. No dial tone. He throws the phone down.*) Damn! They've cut off the line. Go immediately. Tell all the foreign directors that today's meeting is canceled. Tell them they mustn't . . . shouldn't leave their stations until further notice. And the General too . . .
(*YOBE, leaving.*)

IKPOBA:

I hear say dem don catch . . . catch . . .

OCEANA:

Who now? Speak?

IKPOBA:
De petrol oga for offshore.

OCEANA:
What? The Director of Mob . . . ?

IKPOBA:
Yes. Dat oga too.

OCEANA:
Bastards? God!

IKPOBA:
Yes. Dem catch am. Dat red oga. De one wey get hair like like . . .
horse . . .
(*Still stunned, YOBE lingers. Like a fish out of water, OCEANA opens his
mouth, closes it again. He is choking. YOBE helps him into a chair, goes
for a drink to calm him down.*)

OCEANA:
(*Sighing.*) God! My God! They got them.

YOBE:
Who knows?

OCEANA:
Who next?

IKPOBA:
(*Fanning OCEANA.*) Oga no worry. I don lock the gate. Dem no go fit
come here. Me I go massacre them, one by one. Oga no worry. I dey for
your side.

YOBE:
Are you sure they kidnapped the Offshore Oil Director?

IKPOBA:
I see am wit my koro-koro eyes like dis. (*He demonstrates.*) Dem beat
am like dis . . . like dem Fulani boys wey dey beat cattle namma . . . wey
no dey gree waka. (*Imaginary whipping.*) Kaaaii!

OCEANA:
What debacle!

IKPOBA:
Oga wetin you talk? Make I dey call Debo Cole?

OCEANA:
Idiot! Get out of my sight. (*Turns to YOBE.*) Does the General know
about this incident already?

YOBE:
Hmmm, not sure. (*Pause.*) It's time for . . . for the SITREP.

OCEANA:

Yes. The situation report!
(*YOBE turns to go.*)

YOBE:

(*To OCEANA.*) I'm so sorry about this.

OCEANA:

Away with your sorrows! I don't need them. Just go. Go tell him now!
(*YOBE stops, sighs heavily.*)

YOBE:

Believe me. We'll do everything in our power to arrest the situation. I
promise. (*Calmly.*) For now, stay home. I'll do whatever is necessary to
bring all the criminals to justice. We're in this together.

OCEANA:

Sure. You're responsible, I know. But . . . but . . . take care . . .

YOBE:

I will. (*Sighs.*) Everything will be over. Soon. See you.

OCEANA:

Soon. Don't be long.

YOBE:

I won't.
(*Exit Government Official. OCEANA begins to puff away at his cigarette,
while he motions to the Guard to follow YOBE on his way to the gate.
Loudly to the Guard.*) It's night already. Lock up and don't let anyone in.

IKPOBA:

(*Saluting.*) Yessaar!

YOBE:

You stay in charge . . . in your post.

IKPOBA:

Yes, saar. (*Smiles, poses proudly.*) Me I dey in charge.

YOBE:

He's a stranger, remember? He's in your hands.

IKPOBA:

Oga. I know. I know. E dey for my hand. Efery tin . . . efery body dey
for my hand now. (*Boasting.*) Me, I dey kwa!

YOBE:

(*Emphatically.*) Then, control. Take care of him.

(The Guard gives him a final salute. YOBE departs. As soon as he's gone, IKPOBA, the Guard, jumps, whistles, and turns off the light. Led by OMI, the militants crawl nearer to their target, OCEANA. OMI positions herself to cut off the light in preparation for OCEANA. As they wait, throbbing drums mixed with loud animal sounds slash through the thick silence. OCEANA stands, groping and confused until the lights snap, followed by a loud, mocking laughter.)

MOVEMENT ELEVEN

(An emergency cabinet meeting in a corner of the Oil Club. Present are YOBE, the Government Official, PIPELINE, the Chief, and the police. They are awaiting the arrival of the General. Masked, OCEANA plays the General here. BONNY plays Police Officer One. IKPOBA plays the role of Police Officer Two.)

YOBE:
What a shame! They got the Deputy Director!

PIPELINE:
My brother. See me, see, trouble-o! *Dis women wan pour san-san for my garri.*

YOBE:
Imagine? Blasted villagers! Want to hold the entire nation for ransom? Just imagine that! *(Heavy sigh.)*

PIPELINE:
Women? I told you. Stubborn. Stubborn goats!
(Bugle sounds interrupt them. OCEANA/GENERAL enters with a stick/staff. They stand at attention.)

OCEANA/GENERAL:
(Furious.) Goats? No room for goats, wild or tame in this administration. *(Shouts.)* Understand?

ALL:
Yes, your Excellency!

OCEANA/GENERAL:
(To PIPELINE.) Now you! What do you know about this riot?

PIPELINE:
(Trembling.) Not . . . your Excellency. Nothing, your Excellency.

OCEANA/GENERAL:
And those rioters are your people. Not so?

PIPELINE:
(Coughs, still shivering.) Ehmmm . . . Oh God. I know. Our enemies . . . *(Rapidly.)* Yes! Our enemies . . . Neighbors.

OCEANA/GENERAL:

I don't care about your damned neighbors! Just tell me what's going on. Why is the whole nation on fire? Tell me why. Or you'll be sorry for . . . !

PIPELINE:

God Almighty!

OCEANA/GENERAL:

Hey, leave God out of this. Tell me who . . . !

PIPELINE:

My General. Those people . . . terrorists . . . enemies . . . want . . . want to ruin us.

OCEANA/GENERAL:

Enemies? Terrorists? Who? Tell me . . . Name?

PIPELINE:

(*Trembling.*) Emm . . . em . . . Women . . . Girls . . . I mean boys. All of them.

OCEANA/GENERAL:

Your people then? You sent . . .

PIPELINE:

No, your Excellency. I didn't. God knows I didn't . . .

OCEANA/GENERAL:

(*Enraged.*) I say leave God out of your bloody business and talk to me! Talk to me. Didn't you send them?

PIPELINE:

Yes, Lord . . . General . . . I mean . . . ehmmm . . . No . . . (*Sighs, stops.*)

OCEANA/GENERAL:

I take it that you have no control over them; your bloody people. And you are the appointed Chief? Why then do you think we pay you? Eh? (*Silence.*) Your salary . . . your chieftaincy title is hereby revoked with immediate effect.

PIPELINE:

(*Alarmed, kneels at the feet of the General.*) Ah . . . ah . . . ah . . . God . . . Gene . . . general . . . I said it. These people . . . the terrorist . . . Wahala . . . Aaaaaah!

YOBE:

And worse still, the deputy . . . Vice Director . . .

OCEANA/GENERAL:

(*Howling.*) His Vice . . . ? My God! What's wrong? Tell me what happened?

YOBE:

Kid . . .

OCEANA/GENERAL:

(*Hysterical.*) Nabbed?

YOBE:

Napped . . . General . . . Kidnapped. That's what I meant.

OCEANA/GENERAL:

Foreign nationals? Partners kidnapped? This country? Nonsense!

YOBE:

Yes, General. Beats me . . .

OCEANA/GENERAL:

And now we can't drill or sell oil. Losses! Losses! And more losses! (*Silence.*) Now let's hear the full report.

YOBE:

(*Nervous.*) Yes, Lord . . . General. (*Reading.*) The nation is in crisis. Some, today, narrowly escaped . . . Ehm! We . . . we'll come to that, General. (*Coughs.*) Our foreign trading partners missing . . . kidnapped. Pipeline's on fire. The villagers demanding more and more ransom everyday. Now they want to be paid in dollars and pound sterling.

OCEANA/GENERAL:

Nonsense!

YOBE:

Yes, Lord. Hear . . . hear it, now. From the horse's mouth.

OCEANA/GENERAL:

(*Yells.*) Yes, Police. Report?

BONNY/POLICE OFFICER ONE:

(*Military salute but frightened.*) Got them . . . two prisoners.

OCEANA/GENERAL:

Great! Continue.

BONNY/POLICE OFFICER ONE:

(*Saluting.*) Yeaa-saaarp! Dangerous criminals. Old women caught them. Prisoners. Yes. (*Takes chains out of his pocket.*) With these. Chained them. Yes. We chained them . . . locked them up.

OCEANA/GENERAL:

Where?

BONNY/POLICE OFFICER ONE:

Maximum security, saar.

OCEANA/GENERAL:
So no problem. (*Orders the other Police Officer.*) Go immediately. Bring the prisoners here. Now!

BONNY/POLICE OFFICER ONE:
(*Salutes, steps forward, stops.*) Saar . . . Oga.

OCEANA/GENERAL:
Why stand there grinning like a goat-head on fire? I say go!

BONNY/POLICE OFFICER ONE:
(*Frightened.*) But saar . . . oga. Not there. The prisoners dis . . . dis . . . nation . . .

OCEANA/GENERAL:
The nation, what? (*Silence.*) Yes, I'm waiting. Tell me. What's happened to the nation?

BONNY/POLICE OFFICER ONE:
Dis . . . disappeared.

OCEANA/GENERAL:
The Nation? Disappeared? Are you out of your mind?

BONNY/POLICE OFFICER ONE:
(*Trembling.*) No . . . mind . . . gone . . . I mean the nation . . .

OCEANA/GENERAL:
Precisely! (*Tense silence, then impatiently.*) Say . . . what's wrong with the nation?

BONNY/POLICE OFFICER ONE:
(*Tries to steady himself.*) Criminals . . . Oga, criminals. Gone!

OCEANA/GENERAL:
What? You let them escape?

BONNY/POLICE OFFICER ONE:
No saar. Dis . . . appear. Disappeared.

OCEANA/GENERAL:
How? What do you mean?

BONNY/POLICE OFFICER ONE:
Two old women . . .

IKPOBA/POLICE OFFICER TWO:
Witches.

OCEANA/GENERAL:
You mean my Government now pays the police to arrest witches?

IKPOBA/POLICE OFFICER TWO:
Oh no . . . (*Saluting.*) Yes, saar!

BONNY/POLICE OFFICER ONE:
(*Pushing the other aside.*) No, saar! He means ... (*Confronting his partner.*) Witch-hunting! Yes, that's what you're doing.

IKPOBA/POLICE OFFICER TWO:
Won't you let me finish?

BONNY/POLICE OFFICER ONE:
No, I won't. (*Saluting.*) Hear, saar. Don't mind him. He's ... he's lost. Crazy, my General. I'll tell you nothing ... nothing but the truth.

OCEANA/GENERAL:
Still waiting.

BONNY/POLICE OFFICER ONE:
As I was saying before he rudely interrupted. We got, chained the prisoners. Shameless old women who instead of staying quietly ... in their homes ...

IKPOBA/POLICE OFFICER TWO:
Graves!

OCEANA/GENERAL:
Now shut up! And let him speak!

IKPOBA/POLICE OFFICER TWO:
(*Saluting.*) Yes, saaar!

OCEANA/GENERAL:
With so many bas ... idiots ... What a country?
(*He freezes, while the other chuckles, resumes his report.*)

BONNY/POLICE OFFICER ONE:
Chained. Chained them. Yes saar. My evidence? I have these chains to prove it, saar. (*Brandishing the chains.*) Here! But then the enemies are powerful ... so powerful. Once we locked them up, they turned into dogs, you know, like those security dogs? (*The General is stunned and simply gives him a glare.*) Well, in the cell, the dogs started barking, barking, crying and wailing ... even like human beings. God ... General. Ah! In all my years, I've never seen or heard dogs bark like that. Those horrifying noises. Sounds that rip your heart open! Ah! So thinking the chains were too tight, we tried to untie ... I mean loosen the chains a bit. Before we knew it, the gods ... I mean, *dogs* were gone. How? Where? When? We don't know. Just the chains. These chains. All we have left. So, what else could we do, my General?

OCEANA/GENERAL:
Shoot! Shoot the blasted dogs. Criminals! That's what you're paid to do as police officers! Kill. Kill. Understand?

POLICE OFFICERS:
(*Saluting.*) Yes, saar.

OCEANA/GENERAL:
So repeat. What did I say?

IKPOBA/POLICE OFFICER TWO:
(*Aims an imaginary gun.*) Shoot! Shoot them!

OCEANA/GENERAL:
On sight. Any time! Any place! At least, if you shoot them . . . dogs . . .
That's all they are . . .

YOBE:
Except these International Civil . . .

OCEANA/GENERAL:
(*Screams.*) Nonsense!

YOBE:
Their rights!

OCEANA/GENERAL:
Lies!

YOBE:
Rights, saar . . . Their rights . . .

OCEANA/GENERAL:
Bull Sh . . . You heard him. He said they're dogs . . . turned gods . . .
I mean . . . how can the state be prosecuted for killing dogs? Mere
dogs, eh!

PIPELINE:
Your Excellency, I understand. But we have to remember that . . . that
this is an elected government . . . by . . . for . . . the people . . . and all
that. You know?

OCEANA/GENERAL:
I don't . . . know a thing. And don't want to know.

PIPELINE:
As democrats . . .

OCEANA/GENERAL:
(*Incensed.*) Rats! That's all! (*Pause, threatening PIPELINE.*) Now, depart!
You, out of my sight!
(*PIPELINE, frightened, runs out. The General begins to pace up and
down, not addressing anyone in particular.*)
And the budget . . . our budget? How are we going to manage? With all

the salary increase already announced? (*Firmly.*) Officials, note this. (*They salute, write.*) No salary will be paid from now on until those people come to their senses! No salary will be paid. Yes! They'll suffer . . . suffer for this. Today, with immediate effect, I declare a state of emergency. Dawn to dusk curfew. Understand?

POLICE OFFICERS:
(*Saluting.*) Yes, saar!

OCEANA/GENERAL:
Go. Mobilize the Division One Brigade.

POLICE OFFICERS:
Yesaaar! Sack the entire village. Shoot at sight!

IKPOBA/POLICE OFFICER TWO:
What?

OCEANA/GENERAL:
I say shoot . . . shoot . . . anyone . . . anything . . . Living or dead. Shoot! Shoot at sight. Anybody. Nobody must be spared.

BONNY/POLICE OFFICER ONE:
Saar. Already, the whole nation . . . I mean, village is under arrest. Old, young . . . everybody. But the girls . . . Only those girls! And those old women? Their ring leaders . . . But we'll get them.

OCEANA/GENERAL:
(*Shouting.*) All! Put all of them in custody!

IKPOBA/POLICE OFFICER TWO:
Your wish is my command! (*He salutes, then marchs out.*)

YOBE:
Your Excellency. We must be cautious. The world . . . the world is watching . . .

OCEANA/GENERAL:
Damn the whole blasted world! I rule . . . command . . .

YOBE:
Hooligan . . . Your Excellency! Just hooligans. Only a few . . . idiots . . . That's the problem.

OCEANA/GENERAL:
Nonsense! Only a handful of terrorists and they're causing us all these damages? And now they're kidnapping our strange . . . I mean foreign business partners! And you know what that means to the image of this country. Shame. Shame! And more shame! (*Pensive.*) And our legacy? Hasn't the nation suffered enough already? (*Silence.*) Who next? Who knows? (*Pause.*) Can't you see? All this embarrassment? International disgrace? And we're only just trying to clean up our messy image before

the whole world? Now these idiots—the so-called activists are going to cry out about human rights abuses? Huh? Nonsense! They better know this. Their rights end where mine begin. Can't they see? Look who's abusing whom now? I'm ready. It's tit for tat. Go! Sack the entire village. Or better still, arrest all the criminals!

YOBE:
A great idea, your Excellency. That's much better.

OCEANA/GENERAL:
So go now and arrest them.

BONNY/POLICE OFFICER ONE:
Who precisely?

OCEANA/GENERAL:
Are you deaf? I said anyone found in that village.

YOBE:
But your Excellency, remember we're being watched. The press . . . The whole world . . .

OCEANA/GENERAL:
Then blindfold them.

YOBE:
The world?

OCEANA/GENERAL:
Stop asking questions! This is our country!

YOBE:
Our democracy.

OCEANA/GENERAL:
Damn demo-crazy! Slows down . . . cripples everything! (*He sighs, paces, then stops. His mood changes.*) OK. Their voice. Yes . . . their voice . . . We must show the world that people cannot take the law into their hands. Yes, we'll show our trading partners that we, too, are a nation of law and order. Criminals must not be allowed to go unpunished.

YOBE:
But their rights too . . .

OCEANA/GENERAL:
I suppose . . . (*Sighs heavily.*) OK. Lock up all the criminals. (*Hitting the ground with his walking stick.*) They will be tried. Everyone!

BONNY/POLICE OFFICER ONE:
The ring leaders are still at large.

OCEANA/GENERAL:
(*Ignoring him.*) Bloody activists making mincemeat of the state . . .

administration . . . Saboteurs! All of them. Maybe they're even being paid by my past . . . I mean the last administration to ruin me. Ha! (*Screaming.*) Go find them! Find them! Bring them to me . . . On their knees. And that's *my* order! Or be stripped of your rank!

BONNY/POLICE OFFICER ONE:
When, saar?

OCEANA/GENERAL:
Now!

BONNY/POLICE OFFICER ONE:
Yes, Lord . . . Excellency. Your will . . . be done.
(*He salutes, marches out. War drums and frenzied music/dance continue throbbing in the near distance. Lights snap.*)

MOVEMENT TWELVE

(As the people organize in the dark, more explosive sounds can be heard. Voices of protesting women and the youths can be heard. They're now ready to attack and they have Oceana's gun. BONNY/GUARD X and the fugitive or jailed women, too, have joined them. Thereafter, OCEANA enters, groping for the light that's since been cut off. Loud drumbeats and explosive sounds take over.)

OCEANA:
Say. What have they done this time? Who? Who took . . . took the light? *(Shouts.)* Guard! *(Silence.)* Security? Lights! *(Silence.)* Lights! *(Silence.)* Security, where are you? What's going on? *(Silence.)*

YOBE:
(Entering.) What's *not* going on?

OCEANA:
(Startled.) My God! You scared me!

YOBE:
(Agitated.) I'm sorry. Crisis. Crisis. Listen, my friend.
(War drums break loose.)

OCEANA:
(Frightened.) They're already here?

YOBE:
No, they're marching . . .

OCEANA:
(Alarmed.) Where?

YOBE:
On the streets.

OCEANA:
They're coming? *(Sighs.)* I'm finished. Hold me. *(They support each other.)*

YOBE:
You're not alone. *(Chanting and drumming intensifies.)*

OCEANA:

(*Frantic.*) Finished. We're finished. (*Pause.*) What are they saying? What do they want?

YOBE:

They say they too can do oil bunkering. They've set the Zone A oil pipeline on fire.

OCEANA:

(*Alarmed.*) What? The new plant?

YOBE:

Yes. (*Rising tension. Sounds of the protesters. OCEANA searches frantically for his gun. But he can't find it. Meanwhile, the protesting women, led by OMI, IMO, and HADEJA, approach with the gun.*)

OCEANA:

Oh my God! My gun! That guard. The bloody thief must have stolen it. I'm gone! Gone!

(*He's still searching for his weapon. Meanwhile, the explosive sounds continue, followed by loud drumbeats. PIPELINE enters.*)

PIPELINE:

(*Running.*) What are you going to do?

YOBE:

You can see there's no time to waste. The General has sent me here to summon you all.

OCEANA:

And we have to go?

PIPELINE:

Do we have a choice?

OCEANA:

I guess not.

YOBE:

No.

(*Silence. They stare at each other.*)

Gentlemen, it's time for us to go.

(*Exit PIPELINE and YOBE. Some of the activists ambush and arrest them. Others, led by OMI and IMO, invade the premises and bind Oceana's hands and feet together as he struggles to be free.*)

OCEANA:

You? You too? But I've been kind to you. Giving you my money?

OMI:

Stolen from our land.

OCEANA:

I see. You will regret this.

OMI:

Re-what? Ha! Ha! Ha! Look at me now, Oceana. Where? Where is your power? (*Displaying her chest.*) Shoot! Shoot! Shoot, Lord Director!

OCEANA:

(*Spitefully.*) I will get you.

OMI:

What? So he still has a mouth? Now get it. First!
(*She slaps him. OCEANA swoons, bleeds.*)

IMO:

No, sister. No blood.

OMI:

Yes. We must avoid violence.

IMO:

Their game. Their style.

OSHIMI:

Yes, children. We must not leave our dance to dance somebody else's dance.
(*They start leading him away. IMO is soothing OCEANA, wiping away the blood.*)

IMO:

Sorry about that, Mr. Oceana Wilbros. Just one of those things . . . with young people. Can anyone stop youthful exuberance?

CROSS RIVER:

Payback time! What you people have done to us . . . to this land? (*Deep sigh.*)

OCEANA:

Not me. I've done nothing.

IMO:

Precisely! You've done nothing. Nothing good for this land.

HADEJA:

Except to take and take and take!

OCEANA:

Look here. I did my part. I'm only here to represent an interest, you know. I'm not part of the system. Your government . . .

IMO:

Your partners in crime.

OMI:

You work with them. You eat with them.

IMO:

Then get ready to die with them! (*Jumps to fight him.*)

OSHIMI:

(*Restraining her.*) Imo. Stop!

IMO:

(*Enraged.*) No, mother! Not now! You see? You know what they did to me?

CROSS RIVER:

To us. We know. But calm. We'll see the light.

OSHIMI:

At the end of the tunnel.

OMI:

(*Rather coyly, takes up Oceana's chin.*) Now, look into my face. Tell me. Tell us. How do you feel now?

OCEANA:

Betrayed. Abandoned.

IMO:

Like us? (*Silence.*)

OSHIMI:

Then you're not alone, man.

CROSS RIVER:

Makes us one. United.

IMO:

So welcome to the Club!

OMI:

Our Club!

CHORUS:

Of sufferers! Welcome, man!

OMI:

(*Like a reporter.*) And tell me, what is it that you want very much now?

OCEANA:

Freedom. I want my freedom.

IMO:

For how much? How much are you willing to pay?

OCEANA:

Pay for what? I owe you nothing!

IMO:

Ha! Ha! Ha! You don't?

OCEANA:

(*Sternly.*) Yes!

IMO:

You'll soon find out.

OCEANA:

Abuse my rights? Ah! You people. You better . . . Better set me free.

IMO:

Just like that? Your freedom, *free?*

HADEJA:

When you people make us pay . . .

BONNY/GUARD X:

For everything . . .

OMI:

Even for the polluted air you make us breathe in this land.

IMO:

Now it's time. Pay!

OCEANA:

So what do you want? How much?

IMO:

Three billion.

OCEANA:

(*Stunned.*) What?

OMI:

The price.

OCEANA:

Ransom.

OMI:

Wrong! Freedom costs.

OCEANA:

Yours . . .

OMI:

Ours!

OCEANA:

You're much too demanding.

OMI:

Really? Your friends know.

IMO:

Ask them. They're waiting.

OCEANA:

(*Pressing the alarm button.*) Ah! They're here! Tell the Chief and the Government Official. Get them. Please get them.

OMI:

For you? Or for us?

OCEANA:

(*Shocked.*) I . . . I . . . thought . . . for me. Where are they?

IMO:

Waiting. (*Calls.*) Hadeja! Where is she?

OMI:

She's already there to take her place.

IMO:

Great girl!

OCEANA:

Please, the Chief. Where's he?

OMI:

In her hands.

OCEANA:

Whose?

OMI:

My sister's. Hadeja. You know her?

OCEANA:

(*Vehemently.*) I don't! What is there to know?

IMO:

The Chief does. You'll know when the time comes.

OCEANA:

When is that?

BONNY/GUARD X:

When you pay.

OCEANA:

Your ransom. How much?

IMO:

We said *three billion.* Now! (*Ready to strike again.*)

OMI:

No, sister. It's not our way.

IMO:

And our ransom?
(*HADEJA erects a banner from which they read aloud.*)

OMI:

Food!

HADEJA:

Good roads! Not potholes!

CROSS RIVER:

Clean water for cooking and drinking!

IMO:

Clean air! Clean environment.

OMI:

Yes. Unpolluted.

IMO:

And electricity?

OMI:

So tell your people that unless they pay, you'll remain our guest.

IMO:

For life! Ha! Ha! Ha!

(*The women join her laughter. They start pulling him away.*)

HADEJA:

Ha, man. Know that you don't just take and take.

CROSS RIVER:

Yes. You give and take.

CHORUS:

That's what life's all about!

HADEJA:

So now it's time to give . . .

CHORUS:

(*Singing and dancing.*) Give back! Give back!

OMI:

That's how to live.

CHORUS:

In freedom! For freedom! Freedom!

OMI:

(*To OSHIMI and CROSS RIVER.*) Thank you, mothers. Go. Leave the rest to us.

IMO:

Yes, mothers. It's up to us now.

OSHIMI AND CROSS RIVER:

We'll still take care.

OMI:

But go. You know they're looking for you. Go now.

IMO:

Mothers, remember your place. Stay in place.

OSHIMI AND CROSS RIVER:

(*Departing.*) Yes, children. Take care.

(*They're still chanting and dancing when the government forces swoop down and arrest OMI, IMO and IKPOBA, the Bandit-Boy. The others escape. Blackout.*)

Epilogue: A Nation in Custody

(Sunrise. Siren sounds mixed with military music. Tension. Barricades as stage opens, revealing the lounge at the Oil Club, now turned Supreme Court and awaiting the trial of the prisoners. The screen shows flashes of a very rowdy mob, struggling to get through the barricades but unable to do so. For a while, their charged voices fill the air: "Free! Free! Free our women! Free! Free! Free the mothers! Free! Free! The Sisters! Free! Free! Say Freeeeeeedooooom!"

PIPELINE/TRIAL JUSTICE is already on stage, trying out robes, ties, and other paraphernalia in preparation for his new role as the Trial Justice. The lounge table has been raised and draped with white cloth. Unknown to them all, the escaped prisoners, OSHIMI and CROSS RIVER have bribed the police officer to take the jailed youths, IMO and OMI, out of the cell. Now, as they await the trial of their people, all the escapees have reorganized and positioned themselves under the draped lounge table, ready to strike. Then suddenly, OCEANA as the General walks in with a swagger and a stick.)

PIPELINE/TRIAL JUSTICE:
(Startled.) My God . . . Your Excellency! Aaaah!

OCEANA/GENERAL:
(Smiling.) Justice Alpha. I didn't mean to scare you, of all people.

PIPELINE/TRIAL JUSTICE:
(Uneasy.) Ehmm . . . OK. Your . . . Ex . . . Just that I wasn't expecting you here.

OCEANA/GENERAL:
I rule this country, you know. Any problem?

PIPELINE/TRIAL JUSTICE:
Ah yes! No. Ehmmm . . . just this mob.

OCEANA/GENERAL:
I know. A nuisance. A great nuisance!

PIPELINE/TRIAL JUSTICE:
Like an itch in the eye?

OCEANA/GENERAL:
Delicate. Quite delicate, I know. (*Pause.*) But at times, one may have to break an eyeball that itches. Not so?

PIPELINE/TRIAL JUSTICE:
Not normally.

OCEANA/GENERAL:
(*Impatiently.*) In military contexts, we do. We have to.

PIPELINE/TRIAL JUSTICE:
(*Smiling.*) Except this is a . . .

OCEANA/GENERAL:
(*Defensively.*) Democratic government . . . as they say. (*Drawing near, confiding in the Justice.*) Look, my friend. I know how you feel . . . Justice, democracy, human rights, and all that cra . . .

PIPELINE/TRIAL JUSTICE:
Not to talk of the fact that the whole world is watching us now.
(*The Justice is now fully robed.*)

OCEANA/GENERAL:
Yes. To see us fail. But we won't. With your cooperation, we won't.

PIPELINE/TRIAL JUSTICE:
Promise.

OCEANA/GENERAL:
All we need is to give the world out there an appearance of justice. I mean fairness.

PIPELINE/TRIAL JUSTICE:
Under the constitution, the suspects . . .

OCEANA/GENERAL:
(*Correcting.*) Criminals!

PIPELINE/TRIAL JUSTICE:
Oh, well. Deemed innocent until . . .

OCEANA/GENERAL:
Proven guilty. I hear.

PIPELINE/TRIAL JUSTICE:
The prisoners deserve a fair trial.

OCEANA/GENERAL:
Granted. (*Brief pause, then raised stern voice.*) Criminals! That's what they are. (*Bitterly.*) These bastards want to ruin me? My regime? Perhaps they're even paid by my opponents and past administration to incite . . . subvert the good progress we're making in this administration?
(*As they speak, the tension outside intensifies.*)

PIPELINE/TRIAL JUSTICE:

And the people's rights? Look, General. The people's right of speech is part of that progress.

OCEANA/GENERAL:

Oh no! Nobody says the people have no rights. But rights must be measured . . . I mean . . . moderated. No, we can't deny that. But what this administration will not tolerate is people defending, I mean taking the law into their hands in the name of rights.

PIPELINE/TRIAL JUSTICE:

Self-protection. Remember.

OCEANA/GENERAL:

(*Passionately.*) Look, Justice. All that I understand. But remember too that nobody is above the law.

PIPELINE/TRIAL JUSTICE:

(*Smiling.*) Precisely! That's why we must put that into practice. Our nation is already so stigmatized before the people, before the international community. Human Rights abuses, massive imprisonment without trial. Now . . .

OCEANA/GENERAL:

(*Impatiently.*) All that must be reversed. And you alone hold the key to all that.

PIPELINE/TRIAL JUSTICE:

How? As a Judge, my job is to try . . .

OCEANA/GENERAL:

(*Closely, passionately.*) The criminals! Saboteurs! Can't you see? I have reports. They're paid. Paid to ruin you . . . and me, I have it here (*He pulls out a list from his files.*). Yes, we are a nation on trial. This must stop. The image of the nation has been beaten, battered, and fried deep in the court of public opinion. Now we must rescue and heal it. You and I. Promise? (*He waits for it to sink in as the Justice stands, weighing his words.*) Is it not obvious? Where? Where has it ever happened that illiterate rural women . . . women and mere girls rise up in arms against elected and established government? Women, militarized? Haba, Judge! Where have you ever heard that? Eh? Look, if they had revolted during the last military democracy . . . I mean . . . military dictatorship, I could . . .

PIPELINE/TRIAL JUSTICE:

Understand . . .

OCEANA/GENERAL:

But trust me. The problem of women's . . . rights? Cancerous growth in the belly of the land. And illiterate women for that matter? How? This has never happened before. I tell you, these women are not acting alone. They're paid rebels. Seditionists . . . As they say, the dancer on the road has a drummer in a nearby bush.

PIPELINE/TRIAL JUSTICE:
True, General. But their rights . . .

OCEANA/GENERAL:
(*Irritated.*) Lies! (*Pause.*) What rights?

PIPELINE/TRIAL JUSTICE:
Women's . . .

OCEANA/GENERAL:
Oh, come on! Don't be fooled by that feminist nonsense. Jargon! Feminists? (*Spits.*) Rabble-rousers! Worst of women. Failed, frustrated women. All of them. Ugly. Old maids. Watch. Watch them. Nowadays when women fail to find husbands, or fail in their marriages, they turn into feminists. Even les . . . bians! (*Spits.*) Abominable! With that, they start spitting fire and hatred against men. And you know, they demonize what they lose, can't reach, or get. That's what the so-called feminists do, if you ask me.

PIPELINE/TRIAL JUSTICE:
(*Stunned.*) Interesting. A most interesting postmodern . . . postpatriarchal ideology. The bottom line is their rights. (*Pause.*) They're masking mourning then?

OCEANA/GENERAL:
All must wait. All rights must come after me . . . I mean my administration. (*Pleads.*) Look, you are a Justice. Execute the women.

PIPELINE/TRIAL JUSTICE:
The law, you mean?

OCEANA/GENERAL:
Yes. Execute all. Everything. Everyone.

PIPELINE/TRIAL JUSTICE:
Without trial?

OCEANA/GENERAL:
Tried. Life sentence? Sure, I'm game. (*Passionately.*) Here. Name your terms. In addition, I will name you to the Supreme Court. (*He waits for his reaction.*) Promise? You are after all, Justice Omega . . . The very best in this land.

PIPELINE/TRIAL JUSTICE:
(*Loud laughter.*) And you the Alpha!

OCEANA/GENERAL:
We stay united. (*Serenading.*) To keep Sufferland one?

PIPELINE/TRIAL JUSTICE:
Is a task that must be done!

OCEANA/GENERAL AND PIPELINE/TRIAL JUSTICE:
All hail Sufferland!

(They both laugh, exchange clapping salute, and embrace. Music swells in the background as the General departs. Immediately the lounge table jerks forward. The women appear in their white shrouds, seize PIPELINE/TRIAL JUSTICE, disrobe him, and quickly bind him, hands and feet. They put ordinary clothes on him, then push him behind. OSHIMI now helps IMO into the gown of the Trial Judge while CROSS RIVER assists HADEJA into the legal outfit of the Defense Lawyer. As the girls adjust to their new roles as Trial Justice and Defense Lawyer, the older women vanish into the crowded community of prisoners. Now the martial sounds. The trial is about to begin as the legal actors take their places at the appropriate moment: BONNY/PROSECUTOR, PIPELINE, the Traditional Chief and OMI, OSHIMI, and CROSS RIVER as the lead prisoners. IKPOBA/POLICE OFFICER TWO takes his position at the court entrance. Outside, the screen shows the screaming, hysterical mob as they march into the courthouse with their victory song: "Onye Akpana nwagu̧ aka no̧du̧! M'O̧dindu̧. M'O̧nwu̧ lanwu̧! Onye akpana nwagu̧ aka no̧du̧!" Lights change as the transformed IMO, acting as the Trial Justice, mounts the legal bench to face the audience who will serve as the jury for this trial. Then IKPOBA/POLICE OFFICER TWO calls out: "All rise!" They obey. "The court is now in session. Let the trial begin," IMO announces. PIPELINE is led to a seat. HADEJA as the defense lawyer now serves him the papers.)

IMO:
(To IKPOBA/POLICE OFFICER TWO.) Bring the prisoners in. *(First, the chained OSHIMI, CROSS RIVER, and OMI are led in.)* The people's Court wishes to declare open the Trial Number 111 of the new Millennium. *(Reading.)* Today, this court will begin with the case of the People against the State.

BONNY/PROSECUTOR:
Your Honor. Point of correction. It's the "State of Sufferland against the People."

IMO:
Do I take it that I'm the Trial Judge here?

BONNY/PROSECUTOR:
Yes, your Honor.

IMO:
And the people are being tried before me?

BONNY/PROSECUTOR:
Yes. But your honor . . .

IMO:

> (*Sternly.*) I will not be interrupted. And if you insist, you will be charged with "Contempt of this Court," Counsel. Understand?

BONNY/PROSECUTOR:

> I do. (*Pause.*) Your Honor, the Bandit-Boy, the ring leader of these people's rebellion is still not here. Do we have your permission to bring him in?

IMO:

> You may.

BONNY/PROSECUTOR:

> (*To IKPOBA/POLICE OFFICER TWO.*) Fetch the criminal here.

IKPOBA/POLICE OFFICER TWO:

> (*Attention and military salute.*) Yessap!
> (*Exit the officer. In no time, IKPOBA returns in chains. With this development, the mob screams: "All Hail Justice! All Hail Freedom!" They drum with their feet, chanting praises to the Bandit-Boy.*)

IMO:

> (*Firmly.*) Order! This is a court of law, not a marketplace! (*Immediate silence.*) Will the plaintiffs present their case? There are numerous charges and countercharges. The People vs. the State.

(*The Prosecutor rises and struts around the space, then takes a stand. For a moment before he speaks, he looks sternly at the prisoners, one by one, chained and arraigned before the court. Meanwhile, HADEJA as Defense Lawyer sits quietly. The Prosecutor takes a roll call of the prisoners, who in turn answer "present."*)

BONNY/PROSECUTOR:

> Omi! Oshimi! Cross River! Ikpoba! (*To the Justice.*) Apart from the fugitive suspects . . .

IMO:

> You have their names?

BONNY/PROSECUTOR:

> Yes, your Honor. Here. (*Reads.*) The State wishes the court to note that some of the dangerous criminals are hereby charged with treason.

IMO:

> (*Writing.*) You know them?

BONNY/PROSECUTOR:

> Women. Two of them, old hags, I should say, are here.
> (*Throws spiteful looks at OSHIMI and CROSS RIVER.*)

IMO:

(*Writing.*) Their names?

BONNY/PROSECUTOR:

Oshimi and Cross River.

IMO:

Will the suspects Oshimi and Cross River stand? (*The prisoners try to stand. But the chains pull them down and they fall. Then rise up painfully again. The Justice begins writing.*) I see. (*Pause.*) You may sit. Counsel, proceed.

BONNY/PROSECUTOR:

Apart from those two who are still at large, your Honor, I present to you the felons. Omi and Ikpoba, popularly known as the Bandit-Boy. These vandals have been tyrannizing the state and its foreign partners for some time now. These criminals have been threatening the peace of the land. Breaking down law and order. Engaging in arson. Kidnapping innocent, law-abiding citizens and foreigners and deriving pleasure from burning down public property. In short, your Honor, these criminals have been charged with a million counts of felonies for their nefarious, irresponsible acts to bring down this proud nation and make it a laughingstock before the global community.

HADEJA:

(*Rising.*) Objection, your Honor. The plaintiff is misleading the court and making provocative, false, malicious, presumptive charges to prejudice the court against my clients.

IMO:

Objection sustained. Counsel, you may proceed.

BONNY/PROSECUTOR:

Your Honor, may I?

IMO:

No. Counsel, be advised to save our time and proceed with your argument.

BONNY/PROSECUTOR:

Hmm . . . Well . . . I now present to this court the abundant evidence before us. (*He shows and circulates pictures of the state casualties.*) As the evidence shows and proves beyond any reasonable doubt, the State hereby charges and insists that these felons be convicted and found guilty on the following counts: Arson, Kidnapping, Assault, Burglary, and Sabotage against national progress. Assembled before you are the plagues afflicting this great nation. And like any pestilence, your Honor, the state is duty-bound to wipe them out before they contaminate and ruin the soul and seed of the land. Therefore, as stipulated in the constitution, under Section 7, Subsection 1998, and as evidenced in the case of Sonny General Against the People, June 8, 1998, we pray to the court that these criminals be executed summarily . . .

HADEJA:

Objection! My learned colleague has chosen to incite, mislead, and manipulate the opinion of this court against my poor clients.

IMO:

Objection sustained. Proceed, Counsel.

BONNY/PROSECUTOR:

Hmm . . . With mounting evidence proved beyond reasonable doubt, these felons deserve Capital Punishment. Or at least to be sentenced to life imprisonment for their atrocious acts against the state, and as a means of healing and restoring the faith and wounded spirit of our land. On these grounds, your Honor, the prosecution will rest its case.

IMO:

(*To the prisoners.*) You have heard the grave charges against you. Do you plead guilty or not guilty?

PRISONERS:

(*Chorus.*) *Not Guilty!*

IMO:

(*Writing.*) The court notes that all the suspects have pleaded *Not Guilty.* Now, Counsel, do you have any witness to testify to your charges?

BONNY/PROSECUTOR:

Oh, yes, your Honor. Many. My witnesses are waiting.

IMO:

They can wait. (*To the Defense Lawyer.*) Does the Defense team have any information for this court at the moment?

HADEJA:

No, your Honor. We can wait. My clients have been waiting. For life. Doing time. But their own time shall come. So we decline to speak at this moment.

IMO:

Then proceed, Counsel.

BONNY/PROSECUTOR:

Thank you, your Honor.

(*He steps out, then calls out for their first witness, "Dr. Oceana! Director of Multinational Oil Club!" Immediately, a tired and frazzled-looking* OCEANA *staggers into the witness box. As soon as he's produced, voices of protest become amplified. The Judge calls for order. The protests die down, and* OCEANA *is made to swear and mount the witness box to give evidence.*)

BONNY/PROSECUTOR:
Please tell your full name to this court.

OCEANA:
My name is Oceana White Western Wilbros.

BONNY/PROSECUTOR:
Your address?

OCEANA:
Crude oil . . . I mean Number One, Onshore Oil Club Villa, the GRA/Oil Club, Sufferland Federation.

BONNY/PROSECUTOR:
What is your professional title and what do you do for a living?

OCEANA:
I am the eminent Director of the International Crude Guild in Sufferland. My business is drilling, selling, buying, and marketing oil to the global community.

BONNY/PROSECUTOR:
What type of oil?

OCEANA:
The Sufferland Crude Sweet.

BONNY/PROSECUTOR:
In what location?

OCEANA:
Inland and offshore as approved and contracted with the government of the land.

BONNY/PROSECUTOR:
Mr. Oceana, please tell this court what you have experienced for some time now in conducting your rightful business?

OCEANA:
In the last two months, especially, I have been molested, harassed, robbed, brutalized. My associates have been kidnapped by these vandals. My personal and company properties continue to be vandalized or stolen. We have experienced unprecedented losses.

BONNY/PROSECUTOR:
Please, Director, give this court an estimate of your loss?

OCEANA:
Billions. This month alone, we have lost more than 10 million dollars.

BONNY/PROSECUTOR:
And?

OCEANA:
And lives. My colleagues . . . members of the cartel . . .

BONNY/PROSECUTOR:
Local or foreign?

OCEANA:
All foreign. Foreigners with rights to decent life and property in this . . . this . . . lawless . . . (*Breaks down. BONNY/PROSECUTOR helps him to his seat.*)

BONNY/PROSECUTOR:
(*To the Court.*) That was . . . is the eminent Dr. Oceana. As you can see, my client has been traumatized, brutalized, and victimized by these criminals, with neither respect for any life nor property. Your Honor, how can anyone with such despicable criminal records be allowed to go free and unpunished? (*Pause.*) Your Honor, at this moment, we'd like to call to the witness box the one called Ikpoba, a lead member of the criminal gang. He's popularly called, "The Bandit-Boy."
(*IKPOBA takes his place on the witness stand.*)
What is your name?

IKPOBA:
Whatever you think or say I am.

BONNY/PROSECUTOR:
What? Answer my question. (*Sternly.*) What is your name?

IKPOBA:
I already said it.
(*BONNY/PROSECUTOR pulls down his glasses below his nose, gives the boy a hard look, and continues.*)

BONNY/PROSECUTOR:
What do you do for a living?

IKPOBA:
Ha! What do I do for a living?

BONNY/PROSECUTOR:
Yes.

IKPOBA:
Am I living? Ha! Ha! Ha!

BONNY/PROSECUTOR:
Well, tell the court.

IKPOBA:
And you think I'm *living*?

BONNY/PROSECUTOR:
Now stop evading the question and . . .

IKPOBA:

Ok. I'll show you.

(*In a swift motion, he gives the lawyer a push, knocks him down to the floor. Quickly, he impounds the man's briefcase and tries to escape as the Judge screams, "Catch him! Catch!" Crowds block his way especially OCEANA, who is suddenly animated.*)

IMO:

Nobody, not even the Prosecutor, is allowed to take the law into his hands. Therefore, the witness is hereby charged with . . .

IKPOBA:

(*Exploding.*) What? Again? It's unfair. You all were here. He asked me to tell the court what I do for a living. And that's what I did. Show him! All I did was his bidding. Obeyed. Showed you just that. What I do for a living. So what else have I done wrong? Where again have I gone wrong? Is there no place, nothing that a poor boy can do right in this land without justice?

BONNY/PROSECUTOR:

My Lord and fellow citizens. You're all witnesses. You've seen it with your very eyes. A hostile witness, with no respect for the rule of law. He is a most dangerous convict, I hereby urge the court to charge him with contempt of court. And more so, sentence him to the firing squad for all his brutal murders of innocent citizens. Nothing more needs be said. The state shall rest its case for now.

IMO:

The court has taken note of your plaintiff's request. And the defendant's position too. This court will rule on this case before proceeding to the others. Until he spoke, the state assumed that everyone had an answer to such a simple question as "What do you do for a living." Well, granted the defendant was too dramatic in response to the question. But then, there is some truth in what he did. To actually *show* what he did for a *living*. And as implied, the defendant contests the assumption that he is living. So what do we mean by living? The defendant has opened up that point of controversy for us to ponder. Are we all living? If so, how? Let me leave it at that. I hereby withdraw my earlier ruling on the defendant's conduct. Let the jury think about it. We shall rule on that later. (*Pause.*) Next?

(*Prosecutor goes to sit down. HADEJA as Defense Lawyer, now rises to take the stand. As soon as she rises, the prisoners chant once again, but IMO halts them.*)

HADEJA:

(*Eloquent, dignified.*) Your Honor. Country men and women. Fellow citizens of the world. And thank you, my learned friend. You have heard the fictional charges cooked up by my learned friend and the powerful in state to annihilate, exterminate a whole community as if they were pests. Now before you all, I present the people. These traumatized people who have been struggling with these powers that beat and keep them down to let them be free, let them have decent jobs. Food. Water. Electricity. Roads. Life. Just the bare minimum for survival. (*Spotlight on each prisoner as she points to them with one hand and holds up a can of insecticide in the other. Then* HADEJA *turns to the jury.*) Just look . . . look at them. Do any of these look to you like mosquitoes?

VOICES:

No!

HADEJA:

Do they look like bugs or pests to you?

VOICES:

No!

HADEJA:

Do they look like animals to you?

BONNY/PROSECUTOR:

Not just animals but beasts. Beasts! (*Voices of protest rise again. The Judge intervenes. The Prosecutor is petrified, screams.*) Is this a trial . . . kangaroo court or . . .

IMO:

(*Firmly.*) Stop! The Prosecutor is hereby fined 1000 bonds for contempt of court. With apologies for questioning the integrity of this court. Now! (*Silence.*)

BONNY/PROSECUTOR:

Your Honor. Is this an inquest? Well . . . ehm . . . Sorry . . . (*Pays fine.*)

IMO:

Counsel, you may now proceed.

HADEJA:

I see. Now we'd like to request that the Prosecutor's witness be brought back here. (OCEANA *is returned to the witness box.* HADEJA *offers the can of insecticide to the Prosecutor, then to* OCEANA.) Here. Take. Feel free. Spray as you have always to pollute the land, the environment. And wipe out anything and anyone in your way . . . outside your interest. (*Silence, as* OCEANA *gazes into space.*) Yes, spray on.

BONNY/PROSECUTOR:

Objection, your Honor! We're being intimidated.

IMO:

Objection overruled! Counsel may proceed.

HADEJA:

For nearly half a century, Your Honor, the living mothers, sons, and daughters of the land have been trampled. Oppressed. Exploited. And dehumanized. You're all witnesses. Since the Sweet Crude was discovered in their land, each one of them has had their own personal tragic experiences. They've been without jobs, farming and fishing resources . . . painful, hard experiences that progressively changed their lives for the worse. My fellow citizens, it is not for me to tell, for as they say, she who wears the shoe knows where it pinches. My learned friend, reinforced by his prosecution witness, has presented these poor women and youths as the nagging pestilence and diseases afflicting this land. Now before you all they stand. Helpless. Poverty-stricken. Shackled. Mothers, sons, and daughters of this land who have become prisoners of the state, foreign and private interests. Here they are. (*Calling.*) Omi! (*As they're called, each prisoner answers "Here!"*) Oshimi! Cross River! Ikpoba! (*Lawyer turns to the jury.*) As you can see, unlike the views of my learned friend—who labels them animals and who neither knows nor calls them by their names—each one of them is fully human; with blood, feeling, emotion, pain. And what more? Every one of them has a name, with meaning, which I don't wish to repeat or dwell on here. See them. They are all living human beings. With equal rights to live. Eat. Make love. Money. And babies and families, just like the rich, mighty, and powerful interests that stifle them. Look. What separates them from you? The only difference continues to be their drying blood, drilled, sapped, plundered, and sold by you, the powerful state and foreign interests, to ensure your gains! With every sale, sapping or siphoning, the people get weaker and weaker and anemic, as you the rich and powerful, suck them dry and get stronger and stronger. At the center of it all? Money! Profit! Power! That, in a nutshell, is the basic difference! The root of the millennium disease in this land. I call it the MPP! Money. Profit. Power. The pandemic! That, my people, is the triple valley separating our world of the poor from the rich. With MPP, our world is carved, sold, and auctioned by the rich and powerful. And today, only two tribes or races exist in our world—the Tribe or Race of the Rich vs. the Poor! Our market culture has emerged. And in this culture, the rich are "colorless." Colorless! In this the poor become imprisoned and sentenced to life by the rich. (*Pause.*) Fellow citizens of the world. I am only an intermediary between the law and the people. I'm only an interpreter of the law. But the people are here. Now. I cannot speak for them. Let them speak. (*To the prisoners.*) Now it's time. Your time. Speak for yourselves! Speak. Who can silence the drums? Sufferland women, speak!

(*The prisoners' voices rise in unison. They stand, holding each other to form a human chain and then raise a chant/dirge that tells their plight. But the Justice soon stops them. OSHIMI stands, weighed down and weakened by her chained arms. In her clenched teeth, she holds the picture of her murdered son and husband, which she tries to wave up and down as she tries to speak.)*

OSHIMI:

Hmmm . . . Hmmmm . . . *(She's trembling, her voice muffled. Sensing her difficulties, the Justice urges her on.)*

IMO:

Speak, Oshimi! It's your time. *(But still overwhelmed by her burden, the woman stumbles and mumbles something again.)*

HADEJA:

Your Honor. As you can see, my clients are weighed down, encumbered by the weight of evidence latched on to their lips. And before I proceed, I pray the court to untie my clients. Free them from the shackles. At least in the democratic world, suspects are presumed innocent until convicted. Not so?

BONNY/PROSECUTOR:

Objection! They're dangerous! They fled, escaped many times from the jail.

IMO:

Objection denied! The Defense is right. *(To the prisoners.)* You are hereby released from your chains. Be untied. Counsel, proceed. *(The prisoners help one another to become untied.)*

HADEJA:

(Gathering all the suspects' pictures.) Your Honor. Here are the exhibits. The tormented faces here to speak for themselves. Do I have the permission of the court to show . . . present the exhibits?

IMO:

You may. *(HADEJA starts circulating the pictures.)*

HADEJA:

Your Honor, shall I request that from now till the end, we reverse the proceedings into an Open Trial.

IMO:

What do you mean?

HADEJA:

In short, your Honor, I propose this. Let the Defendants directly interrogate the prosecution . . . the prosecution witnesses.

IMO:

If you may.

BONNY/PROSECUTOR:

Objection!

IMO:

Denied! The defense can go on.

HADEJA:

Thank you, your Honor. (*To the prisoners.*) It's time now. Speak.

OSHIMI:

(*Sighs heavily, then her lips break loose.*) My people, my name is
Oshimi. I am the leader of the market women. I used to be strong, beau-
tiful. See me now. See what I have become because of what they have
dome to me. To us. Abused. Mother raped. Daughter raped. And raped.
Son slaughtered. Husband roasted. Alive. (*Sighs heavily.*) My body
aches. My heart bleeds. But I'm not alone. Though we suffer together,
each one of us here do have our own scars. Scars. Scars telling our own
peculiar stories. (*Silence.*) Our stories are so long that if we all were to
speak and tell the world all that we have been through, our narratives
would never end. So now, we can only share with you a bite. Just a small
bite as evidence of what eats deep within us. (*Raised voice.*) Mothers,
sons, and daughters of Oilland, do I speak your voice?

CHORUS OF PRISONERS:

Yes!

OSHIMI:

Did you elect me your representative?

CHORUS OF PRISONERS:

Yes!

OSHIMI:

Should I speak our collective voices?

CHORUS OF PRISONERS:

Yes!

OSHIMI:

(*She asks to lift the released photo.*) Look at those pictures again. My
hero. My burden. That was my husband. The father of my children. This
too was my son, bubbling with flesh and blood. Do they not look strong?
Handsome? Respectable? (*Silence.*) But where are they now? (*Silence.*)
Where! (*Silence.*) Can I ask the White man, the General, and the Chief,
together with their friend the mouthpiece of the state. Where? Where is
my husband? And my son? Where? Where are the men? (*Silence.*) Oga,
why do you remain silent? You took my son and husband. (*Passionately.*) Took them. My love. My life. You know what you did with them.
Why? Why? Why do you kill innocent men, women, and children?
Why? (*To the prisoners.*) You are now free. Let the world hear your stories. Tell your stories. Who can silence the drums? Sufferland women
speak! (*Immediately, their tongues break loose as each one speaks his*

or her pain, experience, and condition. This is not scripted but impro-
vised and enacted to reflect each person's uniqueness and creativity,
even as they build into a chorus.)

CHORUS OF PRISONERS:
Why? Why? Why?

OSHIMI:
Tell the world why?

CHORUS OF PRISONERS:
Why? Why? Why?

OSHIMI:
Speak, you rich and powerful men who ride on the painful back of others. Speak! You who drink and dine on the blood of others. What you
did. Why you did . . .

CHORUS OF PRISONERS:
Why? Why? Why?
(*No longer able to keep silent and take the trauma, Oceana's lips break
loose.*)

OCEANA:
I didn't!

OSHIMI:
So who did it?

OCEANA:
Ask the state . . . Your representatives. I am not responsible. I paid. Paid
dearly for all I got.

OSHIMI:
When? To whom? How much?

OCEANA:
It's not for me to say. However little, we paid either what we were told
was due or what it was worth.

OSHIMI:
And that is?

OCEANA:
Nothing . . . Nothing I can say . . .

CHORUS:
Tell! Tell us! Tell now. The world is waiting!

OCEANA:
I paid not only to the middleman . . . businessman, the government, but
the leaders. *Your* leaders . . .

CHORUS OF PRISONERS:
Who?

OCEANA:
Your leaders . . . (*Hesitates.*) The Government Official and the Chief,
for example.

CHORUS OF PRISONERS:
Ohooo! The Thief! We want them! We want justice! Bring the so-called
leaders! Here! Here! Here! Let them speak!

IMO:
Now is the time. (*To the Defense Lawyer.*) Shall we have the Chief and
his friend?

BONNY/PROSECUTOR:
Objection! The Chief is our Prosecution witness.

IMO:
Overruled! Let justice take its course. Bring the witness here. (*In anger,
the Prosecutor stages a dignified walkout.*)

(*Quickly, PIPELINE, the Chief and YOBE, the Government Official go into
the witness box. OSHIMI steps down from the witness box. Quite unex-
pectedly, IMO, steps out of her role and is in place to lead the interro-
gation of the witnesses.*)

IMO:
Will the Defense please allow this bench a few helpful questions.

HADEJA:
(*Stepping aside.*) You have the floor, your Honor.

IMO:
(*To OCEANA.*) White man, repeat your charges against these people.

OCEANA:
I have no charges against them. All I said is that I paid them, each of
them at different times for different things.

IMO:
Like what precisely?

OCEANA:
The farmlands.

IMO:
Ahh! To *whom* did you pay?

OCEANA:
(*Stuttering.*) Your Honor, must I . . . ? Must I answer these people?
They're . . . they're . . .

IMO:

(*Smiling.*) Human beings! People with a voice to speak and ask questions for themselves. They too have the permission of the court to speak. (*To the Defense Lawyer.*) Proceed with your questions.

PIPELINE:

(*Aside, to* YOBE.) These terrible women. Everywhere you are, you meet them coming. You meet them going.

OCEANA:

For example, I paid the Chief for the farmlands.

IMO:

(*Breaking into mock laughter.*) Chief *Thief!* Ha! Ha! Ha! Chief. Did you hear that? (*Silence.*) What do you have to say for yourself? Now defend yourself.

PIPELINE:

(*Vexed.*) I have done nothing to deserve . . .

IMO:

Any good or justice. But you took money from him. For what?

PIPELINE:

For services rendered.

IMO:

Ahaaah! Services! Paid services! To whom? For whom?

PIPELINE:

The people.

IMO:

Whose people?

PIPELINE:

My people.

IMO:

(*Indicating herself.*) Including this one? (*Silence.*) Yes, Chief. Father of the people. Defender of the land. Do you remember this face?
(*IMO takes off her wig and other camouflage. She approaches the Chief. He is stunned, terrified.*)

PIPELINE:

O . . . M . . . !!!! Ha-ha-ha! (*Silence.* PIPELINE *is horrified by the sight of the scarified woman before him.*)

IMO:

Yes. Imo. The same one you sold.

PIPELINE:

(*Gasping.*) What? Is this . . . what ? What happened . . . what did they do to you?

IMO:

No, Uncle . . . Father. It's not others who did it to me. To us. But you.

PIPELINE:

Me?

IMO:

Yes! You father! Burnt me. Raped me!

HADEJA:

(*Stripping her own mask.*) Raped me too!

(*PIPELINE recognizes her too, falls as he grips them both. OMI now joins them.*)

CHORUS OF WOMEN:

(*Chanting.*) Yes, let our daughters speak! Speak for us!

IMO, OMI, AND HADEJA:

(*To OCEANA and YOBE.*) And you too? Remember? See? See your bloody handiwork?

(*The men are stupefied. The women and youths have risen into choral chants. The drumbeats rise slowly. PIPELINE, YOBE, and OCEANA are trembling.*)

PIPELINE:

(*To OCEANA.*) But . . . but . . . I gave you . . .

YOBE:

Oh God! Oh God!

OCEANA:

Save! Save me!

PIPELINE:

(*Gasping.*) Forgive . . . daughters! Sisters, forgive! Never! Never again! I shouldn't . . . shouldn't have . . . My people! I failed . . . failed to defend . . .

YOBE:

If we had to do it all over?

OCEANA:

It will never be the same.

YOBE:

Now we know.

PIPELINE:

Oh yes, we know. (*Delirious, muttering.*) Forgive . . . Forgive . . . Forgive . . .

OCEANA:

We need . . . need . . . talk. Let's talk . . .

YOBE:

Yes. We'll create jobs.

PIPELINE:

Pay you.

OCEANA:

Compensation.

CHORUS OF THE PEOPLE:

We must have our resource! Resource Control! Resource Control!

OMI:

About time!

IMO:

All we ask of you is just to live. Live with dignity in life. And that's what these women and youths have always wanted. But no. In your own way, you stand in their way. In my way. In everybody's way. Because you have the power and the money. Is it fair? Where did we go wrong?

CHORUS OF THE PEOPLE:

Where? Where did we go wrong? What did we do wrong?

OMI:

Is poverty a crime?

IMO:

Is it?

CHORUS:

Is it? Is poverty-poverty a crime!

IMO AND OMI:

(*To their target.*) You tell us.

CHORUS:

Tell us—tell us—tell us . . . Is poverty a crime?

OMI:

Is it?

CHORUS:

Is it? Is it? Is *it*?

IMO:

And so she said it!

CHORUS:

She said it—Said it—What Mama Said. (*Pause.*) *Is it*?

(*With spotlights on them in this call-response chant, the rousing drum-beats empower the women and youths into a huge orchestra as they shift out of the stage and into the audience, to build into a communal dance party until floodlights.*)

BOOKS IN THE AFRICAN AMERICAN LIFE SERIES

Coleman Young and Detroit Politics: From Social Activist to Power Broker, by Wilbur Rich, 1988

Great Black Russian: A Novel on the Life and Times of Alexander Pushkin, by John Oliver Killens, 1989

Indignant Heart: A Black Worker's Journal, by Charles Denby, 1989 (reprint)

The Spook Who Sat by the Door, by Sam Greenlee, 1989 (reprint)

Roots of African American Drama: An Anthology of Early Plays, 1858–1938, edited by Leo Hamalian and James V. Hatch, 1990

Walls: Essays, 1985–1990, by Kenneth McClane, 1991

Voices of the Self: A Study of Language Competence, by Keith Gilyard, 1991

Say Amen, Brother! Old-Time Negro Preaching: A Study in American Frustration, by William H. Pipes, 1991 (reprint)

The Politics of Black Empowerment: The Transformation of Black Activism in Urban America, by James Jennings, 1992

Pan Africanism in the African Diaspora: An Analysis of Modern Afrocentric Political Movements, by Ronald Walters, 1993

Three Plays: The Broken Calabash, Parables for a Season, and The Reign of Wazobia, by Tess Akaeke Onwueme, 1993

Untold Tales, Unsung Heroes: An Oral History of Detroit's African American Community, 1918–1967, by Elaine Latzman Moon, Detroit Urban League, Inc., 1994

Discarded Legacy: Politics and Poetics in the Life of Frances E. W. Harper, 1825–1911, by Melba Joyce Boyd, 1994

African American Women Speak Out on Anita Hill–Clarence Thomas, edited by Geneva Smitherman, 1995

Lost Plays of the Harlem Renaissance, 1920–1940, edited by James V. Hatch and Leo Hamalian, 1996

Let's Flip the Script: An African American Discourse on Language, Literature, and Learning, by Keith Gilyard, 1996

A History of the African American People: The History, Traditions, and Culture of African Americans, edited by James Oliver Horton and Lois E. Horton, 1997 (reprint)

Tell It to Women: An Epic Drama for Women, by Osonye Tess Onwueme, 1997

Ed Bullins: A Literary Biography, by Samuel Hay, 1997

Walkin' over Medicine, by Loudelle F. Snow, 1998 (reprint)

Negroes with Guns, by Robert F. Williams, 1998 (reprint)

A Study of Walter Rodney's Intellectual and Political Thought, by Rupert Lewis, 1998

Ideology and Change: The Transformation of the Caribbean Left, by Perry Mars, 1998

"Winds Can Wake Up the Dead": An Eric Walrond Reader, edited by Louis Parascandola, 1998

Race and Ideology: Language, Symbolism, and Popular Culture, edited by Arthur Spears, 1999

Without Hatreds or Fears: Jorge Artel and the Struggle for Black Literary Expression in Colombia, by Laurence E. Prescott, 2000

African Americans, Labor, and Society: Organizing for a New Agenda, edited by Patrick L. Mason, 2001

The Concept of Self: A Study of Black Identity and Self-Esteem, by Richard L. Allen, 2001

What the Wine-Sellers Buy Plus Three: Four Plays by Ron Milner, 2001

Looking Within/Mirar adentro: Selected Poems, 1954–2000 by Nancy Morejón, 2002

Liberation Memories: The Rhetoric and Poetics of John Oliver Killens, by Keith Gilyard, 2003

What Mama Said: An Epic Drama, by Osonye Tess Onwueme, 2003

For an updated listing of books in this series, please visit our Web site at http://wsupress.wayne.edu